Ruskin Bond is known for his signature simplistic and witty writing style. He is the author of several bestselling short stories, novellas, collections, essays and children's books; and has contributed a number of poems and articles to various magazines and anthologies. At the age of 23, he won the prestigious John Llewellyn Rhys Prize for his first novel, *The Room on the Roof.* He was also the recipient of the Padma Shri in 1999, Lifetime Achievement Award by the Delhi Government in 2012 and the Padma Bhushan in 2014.

Born in 1934, Ruskin Bond grew up in Jamnagar, Shimla, New Delhi and Dehradun. Apart from three years in the UK, he has spent all his life in India and now lives in Landour, Mussoorie, with his adopted family.

RUSKIN BOND

Old Times' Sake

Dear Avery
Enjoy this book from India!
Best wishes
Abeer

RUPA

Published by
Rupa Publications India Pvt. Ltd 2024
7/16, Ansari Road, Daryaganj
New Delhi 110002

Sales centres:
Bengaluru Chennai
Hyderabad Jaipur Kathmandu
Kolkata Mumbai Prayagraj

This is a work of fiction. Names, characters, places and incidents are either the product of the author's imagination or are used fictitiously and any resemblance to any actual person, living or dead, events or locales is entirely coincidental.

P-ISBN: 978-93-6156-686-8
E-ISBN: 978-93-6156-947-0

First impression 2024

10 9 8 7 6 5 4 3 2 1

Printed in India

CONTENTS

INTRODUCTION

Even as one goes through life looking towards the future, the past always has a seductive kind of pull. Every once in a while, one has the desire to pull out an old photo album, play an old favourite song, or simply close one's eyes and reminisce about a time long gone. The images might be blurry, the conversations half-remembered, but the feelings and sensations never fade away.

Old Times' Sake brings together some of my writings in which I have attempted to recount these sensations, rescuing them from the ravages of time. 'The Old Gramophone' and 'In Grandfather's Garden' capture some memories of the simple joy that came from spending time with my grandparents as a child. 'Friends of My Youth' and 'Remember the Old Road' are my odes to friendships, which, even if they don't survive the test of time, remain alive in some corner of one's heart throughout one's life. In contrast to these, I have also included stories like 'Coming Home to Dehra', which recounts a difficult period in my life, as the past is made up of as many painful moments as happy ones.

While not everyone finds nostalgia worthwhile, as a writer I have often dipped into the reserves of my memories to draw out my own observations of human nature and life. Joy is hard enough to come by as it is; if a few moments of dwelling on the past can bring one happiness, then perhaps the occasional indulgence can't be so bad. I hope the stories herein help you look back at your own memories, the good and the bad, allowing you a moment of perspective. For old times' sake.

Ruskin Bond

TALES OF OLD MUSSOORIE

At one time visitors to Mussoorie frequently found themselves persuaded to climb to the top of a local peak called 'Gun Hill', from which one is able to obtain a view of the greater Himalayas. Today a cable car takes tourists to the top of the hill, from which, besides the snows, Mussoorie waterworks, too, can be seen; but of a 'gun' there is no sign, and they may be pardoned for wondering how the hill acquired its impressive name. We hope to enlighten them on this, and other aspects, of the hill station's distant though not ancient past.

Before 1919, noon-time was indicated by the firing of a cannon from the top of 'Gun Hill', possibly because cannons were cheaper than clocks in those days. At first the gun faced east; then soon after its installation, a complaint came from the Grey Castle Nursing Home that the gun when fired 'often let loose plaster from the ceiling of the wards, which fell on patients' beds and unnerved them'. It could not be pointed north because it would then have blasted away a house called 'Dilkush'; so it was faced north-east, but that again couldn't be made its permanent position, for the Crystal Bank then complained. Turned to the south, it almost succeeded in fulfilling its legitimate duty, but that was before the gunner forgot to remove the ramrod from the barrel, and on booming noon to the populace, the cannon sent the ramrod clean through the roof of the Savoy hotel.

Public opinion consequently was mounting against the gun, and it was turned around once more to face the Mall. The boom was usually produced by ramming down the barrel a mixture of moist grass and cotton waste, after the powder was in place. Due to an accidental overcharge of powder, one of these cannonballs landed with some force right in the lap of a lady who was being taken along the Mall in a rickshaw. It was the last straw or, to be exact, the last cannonball, for the gun was dismantled soon after the incident.

A peep into the life of the hill station before the turn of the century is a fascinating exercise; but before giving the reader further anecdotes, we should fill in the background with a brief historical sketch of the hill station.

In the year 1825, the superintendent of the Doon was a certain Mr Shore, who occasionally found time from his official duties to scramble up the range, then known as 'Mansuri' because of the prevalence of a shrub known in the vernacular as the Mansur plant. He found that the range had a number of 'flats', some of which accommodated the huts of cowherds who grazed their cattle on them during the summer months. The hills were then well forested and game plentiful; so the first construction was a shooting-box built jointly by Mr Shore and Captain Young of the Sirmur Rifles. It has long since disappeared, but is said to have been located on the Camel's Back, facing north. The first home—still recognizable—was 'Mullingar' in Landour, built in 1826 by Captain Young. Landour soon became a convalescent depot for British troops; the old convalescent hospital now forms the nucleus of the offices of the Defence Institute of Work Study. Soon civilians were flocking to Mussoorie, building houses as far apart as 'Cloud End' to the west and 'Dahlia Bank' to the east, separated by some twelve miles. In 1832, Colonel Everest (after whom the mountain is named) as Surveyor-General opened his Survey of India office in 'The Park' and made a road to it.

People came to Mussoorie for health, business and pleasure, and amongst the pleasure-seekers we find the Hon'ble Emily Eden, sister of Lord George Eden, Earl of Auckland, Governor General of India. One of our earliest visitors, she records in her famous diaries that 'in the afternoon we took a beautiful ride up to Landour, but the paths are very narrow on that side, and our courage somehow oozed out, and first we came to a place where they said, "This was where poor Major Blundell and his pony fell over and they were both dashed to atoms," and then there was a board stuck in a tree, "From this spot a private in the Cameroons fell and was killed..." We had to get off our ponies and lead them, and altogether I thought much of poor Major Blundell. It is impossible to imagine more beautiful scenery'.

Though there were no proper roads in Mussoorie in those early days, some of the cliff-edge accidents were undoubtedly caused by the beer that was then so cheap and plentiful in the hill station.

Mr Bohle, one of the pioneers of brewing in India, started the 'Old Brewery' near Hathipaon in 1830. Two years later he got into trouble for supplying beer to soldiers who were alleged to have presented forged passes. Mr Bohle was called to account by Captain (by now Colonel) Young for distilling spirits without a license, and had to close his concern. Undaunted, he was back in 1834, building 'Bohle's Brewery', and became a popular figure in Mussoorie society. His tomb in the Camel's Back cemetery is still one of the most impressive.

Scandal again erupted in the brewery business in 1876, when everyone suddenly started talking of a much improved brew. It came from Vat 42 in Whymer and Company's 'Crown Brewery'. The beer was retasted until the diminishing level of the barrel revealed the perfectly brewed remains of a human! Someone had fallen into the vat and been drowned, and, all unknown to himself, had given the beer-trade a real fillip. The author of *A Mussoorie Miscellany* (H.C. Williams) informs us that 'meat was thereafter recognized as the missing component and scrupulosuly added till more modern, and less cannibalistic, means were discovered to satiate the froth-blower'.

A bold, bad place was Mussoorie in those days, according to the correspondent of the *Statesman,* who, in his paper of 22 October 1884, wrote 'Ladies and gentlemen, after attending church, proceeded to a drinking shop, a restaurant adjoining the library, and there indulged freely in pegs, not one but many, and at a Fancy Bazaar held this season, a lady stood up on her chair and offered her kisses to gentlemen at five rupees each. What would they think of such a state of society at home?'

Fifty years later, a Mussoorie lady auctioned a single kiss for 300 rupees. A vivid illustration of the inflationary process throughout history.

But inspite of such goings-on, or perhaps because of them, the inhabitants were conscious of their spiritual needs, and a number of churches were soon dotted about the hill station, the oldest of them being Christ Church (1836).

When, in March 1905, Her Royal Highness the Princess of Wales (later Queen Mary) visited Mussoorie, she planted a deodar tree outside Christ Church. The plaque commemorating this event can still be seen, now almost embedded in the trunk of the tree.

Some thirty years later, the chaplain of Christ Church was the fair-minded Reverend T.W. Chisolm. In his usual Sunday service prayers, in the year 1933, he sought god's help for veteran Indian leader and freedom-fighter, Pandit Motilal Nehru, a regular visitor to Mussoorie, who was then seriously ill. There was an immediate hullaballoo in all official tea sessions, and the chaplain was reprimanded. This caused him to comment, 'That in these years of our Lord, Holy Orders can be interpreted to mean wholly Government orders.'

It is easy enough to get to Mussoorie today, but how did visitors manage it before the advent of the railway and the motorcar? It was surely a difficult exercise. Mr Shore and Captain Young merely scrambled up the goat tracks to get here, and Lady Eden used her pony to canter along paths and 'up precipices'; but before that, one detrained at Ghaziabad (near Delhi), engaged a bullock cart or tonga, and then proceeded in the direction of the Himalayas as speedily as only a bullock cart or tonga could go. After that, one either walked, rode a pony, or was carried uphill in a doolie, a crude sort of palanquin.

By the turn of the century, the 'Sind, Punjab and Delhi Railway' had got as far as Saharanpur, and the bullock cart had given way to the *dak-ghari*.

The only way to reach Dehradun, en route to Mussoorie, was by the dak-ghari or 'night-mail'.

Dak-ghari ponies were different animals, 'always attempting to turn around and get into carriage with the passengers,' as one disgruntled traveller described them. It was only when the coachman used his whip liberally and reviled the ponies' ancestors as far back as three or four generations that the beasts could be persuaded to move. And once they started, there was no stopping them; it was a gallop all the way to the first stage, where the ponies were changed to the accompaniment of a bugle blown by the coachman in true Dickensian fashion.

The journey through the Siwaliks really began—as it still does—at the Mohand Pass. The ascent starts with a gradual gradient, which increases as the road becomes more steep and winding. The hills are abrupt and perpendicular on the southern side, but slope gently away to the north.

At this stage of the journey, drums were beaten (if it was daytime) and torches were lit (if it was night), because frequently wild elephants resented the approach of the dak-ghari and, trumpeting a challenge, would throw the ponies into panic and confusion and send them racing back to the plains.

The railway reached Dehradun in 1901. Till then the main overnight stop was at Rajpur, and the well-known hostelries and forwarding agencies at Rajpur were the 'Ellenborough Hotel', the 'Prince of Wales Hotel', and the 'Agency Retiring Rooms' of Messrs Buckle and Company's 'Bullock Train Agency'. They have long since disappeared. As Dehradun grew in importance, Rajpur's importance dwindled, and for many years its long winding bazaar resembled a ghost town.

Soon the Savoy and Charleville Hotels opened. Massive furniture, grand pianos, billiard tables, barrels of cider and crates of champagne had all come up the hill in lumbering bullock carts. In 1909, the hotels were suddenly ablaze with light, for this was the year when electricity came to Mussoorie. Before that, the ballrooms and dining rooms had been hung with chandeliers, the rooms lit by candlelight, and the kitchens with spirit lamps.

It was after World War I in the 'gay twenties' that the Charleville and the Savoy entered the most popular era, when they were to be as well-known as Raffles in Singapore or the Imperial in Tokyo. Wealthy Indian princes and their families and staff occupied entire wings of the Savoy Hotel. The Savoy Orchestra played every night, and the ballroom was full of couples doing the tango or fox-trot, the latest dancing craze of those days.

After India's Independence in 1947, Mussoorie went through a difficult period. The British had gone, and the wealthy princes and landowners were also finding times difficult. Hotels and boarding houses began to close down. Then, in the early sixties, the prosperous Indian middle classes became hill-station conscious, and once again crowds thronged the Mall on summer evenings. These days the foreign tourist is discovering the delights of the lower Himalayas.

Those who wish to move further into the mountains, either on foot or by road, have a wealth of flora and fauna to discover and enjoy. One of the remarkable features of the Himalayas is the abruptness with which they rise from the plains, and this gives them a verdure that is totally different from that of the plains.

None of the common trees of the plains are to be found in the hills. At elevations of 4,000 ft, the long-leaved pine appears. From 5,000 ft there are several kinds of evergreen oak, and above 6,000 ft you find rhododendron, deodar, maple, the hill crypress, and the beautiful horse-chestnut. Still higher up, the silver fir is common, but at 12,000 ft the firs become stunted and dwarfed, and the birch and juniper replace them. At this height raspberries grow wild, amongst yellow colt's-foot dandelion, blue gentian, purple columbine, anemone and edelweiss.

Not every hillside is covered with foliage. Many hills are bare and rugged, too precipitous for cultivation. Sometimes they are masses of quartz, limestone or granite.

Just as the trees of the plains differ from those of the hills, so do the animals and birds. The bear, the goral (a goat-like animal), the marten, the civet cat, the snow leopard, and the musk deer, all belong to the Himalayas. The caw of the house crow is replaced by the deeper note of the corby, and the melodious green hill pigeon takes the place of the small brown dove.

You do not always see the birds, but you can hear them. As you trek in the interior or wander along a quiet road in the hill station, the sound of birds is very pleasant to hear; just as the sound of water in the valleys, the singing of the hill people, the smell of the pines, and the blue smoke rising from the villages are always with you in the Himalayas.

REMEMBER THE OLD ROAD

Remember the old road,
The steep stony path
That took us up from Rajpur,
Toiling and sweating
And grumbling at the climb,
But enjoying it all the same.
At first the hills were hot and bare,
But then there were trees near Jharipani
And we stopped at the Halfway House
And swallowed lungfuls of diamond-cut air.
Then onwards, upwards, to the town,
Our appetites to repair!

Well, no one uses the old road any more.
Walking is out of fashion now.
And if you have a car to take you
Swiftly up the motor road
Why bother to toil up a disused path?
You'd have to be an old romantic like me
To want to take that route again.
But I did it last year,
Pausing and plodding and gasping for air—
Both road and I being a little worse for wear!
But I made it to the top and stopped to rest

And looked down to the valley and the silver stream
Winding its way towards the plains.
And the land stretched out before me, and the years fell away,
And I was a boy again,
And the friends of my youth were there beside me,
And nothing had changed.

FRIENDS OF MY YOUTH

1
SUDHEER

Friendship is all about doing things together. It may be climbing a mountain, fishing in a mountain stream, cycling along a country road, camping in a forest clearing, or simply travelling together and sharing the experiences that a new place can bring.

On at least two of these counts, Sudheer qualified as a friend, albeit a troublesome one, given to involving me in his adolescent escapades.

I met him in Dehra soon after my return from England. He turned up at my room saying he'd heard I was a writer and asking if I had any comics to lend him.

'I don't write comics,' I said; but there were some comics lying around, left over from my own boyhood collection, so I gave these to the lanky youth who stood smiling in the doorway, and he thanked me and said he'd bring them back. From my window I saw him cycling off in the general direction of Dalanwala.

He turned up again a few days later and dumped a large pile of new-looking comics on my desk. 'Here are all the latest,' he announced. 'You can keep them for me. I'm not allowed to read comics at home.'

It was only weeks later that I learnt he was given to pilfering comics and magazines from the town's bookstores. In no time at all, I'd become a receiver of stolen goods!

My landlady had warned me against Sudheer and so had one or two others. He had acquired a certain notoriety for having been expelled from his school. He had been in charge of the library, and before a consignment of newly acquired books could be registered and library stamped, he had sold them back to the bookshop from which they had originally been purchased. Very enterprising but not to be countenanced in a very *pukka* public school. He was now studying in a municipal school too poor to afford a library.

Sudheer was an amoral scamp all right, but I found it difficult to avoid him, or to resist his undeniable and openly affectionate manner. He could make you laugh. And anyone who can do that is easily forgiven for a great many faults.

One day he produced a couple of white mice from his pockets and left them on my desk.

'You keep them for me,' he said. 'I'm not allowed to keep them at home.'

There were a great many things he was not allowed to keep at home. Anyway, the white mice were given a home in an old cupboard, where my landlady kept unwanted dishes, pots and pans, and they were quite happy there, being fed on bits of bread or *chapatti*, until one day I heard shrieks from the storeroom, and charging into it, found my dear stout landlady having hysterics as one of the white mice sought refuge under her blouse and the other ran frantically up and down her back.

Sudheer had to find another home for the white mice. It was that or finding another home for myself.

Most young men, boys and quite a few girls used bicycles. There was a cycle hire shop across the road, and Sudheer persuaded me to hire cycles for both of us. We cycled out of town, through tea gardens and mustard fields, and down a forest road until we discovered a small, shallow river where we bathed and wrestled on the sand. Although I was three or four years older than Sudheer, he was much stronger, being about six feet tall and broad in the shoulders. His parents had come from Bhanu, a rough-and-ready district on the North West Frontier, as a result of the partition of the country. His father ran a small press situated behind the Sabzi Mandi and brought out a weekly newspaper called *The Frontier Times.*

We came to the stream quite often. It was Sudheer's way of playing truant from school without being detected in the bazaar or at the cinema. He was sixteen when I met him, and eighteen when we parted, but I can't recall that he ever showed any interest in his school work.

He took me to his home in the Karanpur bazaar, then a stronghold of the Bhanu community. The Karanpur boys were an aggressive lot and resented Sudheer's friendship with an *angrez.* To avoid a confrontation, I would use the back alleys and side streets to get to and from the house in which they lived. Sudheer had been overindulged by his mother, who protected him from his father's wrath. Both parents felt I might have an 'improving' influence on their son, and encouraged our friendship. His elder sister seemed more doubtful. She felt he was incorrigible, beyond redemption, and that I was not much better, and she was probably right.

The father invited me to his small press and asked me if I'd like to work with him. I agreed to help with the newspaper for a couple of hours every morning. This involved proofreading and editing news agency reports. Uninspiring work, but useful.

Meanwhile, Sudheer had got hold of a pet monkey, and he carried it about in the basket attached to the handlebar of his bicycle. He used it to ingratiate himself with the girls. 'How sweet! How pretty!' they would exclaim, and Sudheer would get the monkey to show them its tricks.

After some time, however, the monkey appeared to be infected by Sudheer's amorous nature, and would make obscene gestures that were not appreciated by his former admirers. On one occasion, the monkey made off with a girl's *dupatta*. A chase ensued, and the dupatta was retrieved, but the outcome of it all was that Sudheer was accosted by the girl's brothers and given a black eye and a bruised cheek. His father took the monkey away and returned it to the itinerant juggler who had sold it to the young man.

Sudheer soon developed an insatiable need for money. He wasn't getting anything at home, apart from what he pinched from his mother and sister, and his father urged me not to give the boy any money. After paying for my boarding and lodging I had very little to spare, but Sudheer seemed to sense when a money order or cheque arrived, and would hang around, spinning tall tales of great financial distress until, in order to be rid of him, I would give him five to ten rupees. (In those days, a magazine payment seldom exceeded fifty rupees.)

He was becoming something of a trial, constantly interrupting me in my work, and even picking up confectionery from my landlady's small shop and charging it to my account. I had stopped going for bicycle rides. He had wrecked one of the cycles and the shopkeeper held me responsible for repairs.

The sad thing was that Sudheer had no other friends. He did not go in for team games or for music or other creative pursuits which might have helped him to move around with people of his own age group. He was a loner with a propensity for mischief. Had he entered a bicycle race, he would have won easily. Forever eluding a variety of pursuers, he was extremely fast on his bike. But we did not have cycle races in Dehra.

And then, for a blessed two or three weeks, I saw nothing of my unpredictable friend.

I discovered later that he had taken a fancy to a young schoolteacher, about five years his senior, who lived in a hostel up at Rajpur. His cycle rides took him in that direction. As usual, his charm proved irresistible, and it wasn't long before the teacher and the acolyte were taking rides together down lonely forest roads. This was all right by me, of course, but it wasn't the norm with the middle-class matrons of small-town India, at least not in 1957. Hostel wardens, other students, and naturally Sudheer's parents, were all in a state of agitation. So I wasn't surprised when Sudheer turned up in my room to announce that he was on his way to Nahan to study at an Inter College there.

Nahan was a small hill town about sixty miles from Dehra. Sudheer was banished to the home of his *mama*, an uncle who was a sub-inspector in the local police force. He had promised to see that Sudheer stayed out of trouble.

Whether he succeeded or not, I could not tell, for a couple of months later I gave up my rooms in Dehra and left for Delhi. I lost touch with Sudheer's family, and it was only several years later, when I bumped into an old acquaintance, that I was given news of my erstwhile friend.

He had apparently done quite well for himself. Taking off for Calcutta, he had used his charm and his fluent English to land a job as an assistant on a tea estate. Here he had proved quite efficient, earning the approval of his manager and employers. But his roving eye soon got him into trouble. The women working in the tea gardens became prey to his amorous and amoral nature. Keeping one mistress was acceptable. Keeping several was asking for trouble. He was found dead early one morning with his throat cut.

2
THE ROYAL CAFE SET

Dehra was going through a slump in those days, and there wasn't much work for anyone—least of all for my neighbour Suresh Mathur, an income tax lawyer, who was broke for two reasons. To begin with, there was not much work going around, as those with taxable incomes were few and far between. Apart from that, when he did get work, he was slow and half-hearted about getting it done. This was because he seldom got up before eleven in the morning, and by the time he took a bus down from Rajpur and reached his own small office (next door to my rooms), or the income tax office a little further on, it was lunchtime and all the tax officials were out. Suresh would then repair to the Royal Cafe for a beer or two (often at my expense) and this would stretch into a gin and tonic, after which he would stagger up to his first-floor office and collapse on the sofa for an afternoon nap. He would wake up at six, after the income tax office had closed.

I occupied two rooms next to his office, and we were on friendly terms, sharing an enthusiasm for the humorous works of P.G. Wodehouse. I think he modelled himself on Bertie Wooster, for he would often turn up wearing mauve or yellow socks, or a pink shirt and a bright green tie—enough to make anyone in his company feel quite liverish. Unlike Bertie Wooster, he did not have a Jeeves to look after him and get him out of various scrapes. I tried not to be too friendly, as Suresh was in the habit of borrowing lavishly from all his friends, conveniently forgetting to return the amounts. I wasn't well off and could ill afford the company of a spendthrift friend. Sudheer was trouble enough.

Dehra, in those days, was full of people living on borrowed money or no money at all. Hence, the large number of disconnected telephone and electric lines. I did not have electricity myself, simply because the previous tenant had taken off, leaving me with outstandings of over a thousand rupees, then a princely sum. My monthly income seldom exceeded 500 rupees. No matter. There was plenty of kerosene available, and the oil lamp lent a romantic glow to my literary endeavours.

Looking back, I am amazed at the number of people who were quite broke. There was William Matheson, a Swiss journalist, whose remittances from Zurich never seemed to turn up; my landlady, whose husband had deserted her two years previously; Mr Madan, who dealt in second-hand cars that no one wanted; the owner of the corner restaurant, who sat in solitary splendour surrounded by empty tables; and the proprietor of the Ideal Book Depot, who was selling off his stock of unsold books and becoming a departmental store. We complain that few people buy or read books today, but I can assure you that there were even fewer customers in the fifties and sixties. Only doctors, dentists and the proprietors of English schools were making money.

Suresh spent whatever cash came his way, and borrowed more. He had an advantage over the rest of us—he owned an old bungalow, inherited from his father, up at Rajpur in the foothills, where he lived alone with an old manservant. And owning a property gave him some standing with his creditors. The grounds boasted of a mango and litchi orchard, and these he gave out on contract every year, so that his friends did not even get to enjoy some of his produce. The proceeds helped him to pay his office rent in town, with a little left over to give small amounts on account to the owner of the Royal Cafe.

If a lawyer could be hard up, what chance had a journalist? And yet, William Matheson had everything going for him from the start, when he came out to India as an assistant to Von Hesseltein, correspondent for some of the German papers. Von

Hesseltein passed on some of the assignments to William, and for a time, all went well. William lived with Von Hesseltein and his family, and was also friendly with Suresh, often paying for the drinks at the Royal Cafe. Then William committed the folly (if not the sin) of having an affair with Von Hesseltein's wife. Von Hesseltein was not the understanding sort. He threw William out of the house and stopped giving him work.

William hired an old typewriter and set himself up as a correspondent in his own right, living and working from a room in the Doon Guest House. At first he was welcome there, having paid a three-month advance for room and board. He bombarded the Swiss and German papers with his articles, but there were very few takers. No one in Europe was really interested in India's five-year plans, or Corbusier's Chandigarh, or the Bhakra Nangal Dam. Book publishing in India was confined to textbooks, otherwise William might have published a vivid account of his experiences in the French Foreign Legion. After two or three rums at the Royal Cafe, he would regale us with tales of his exploits in the Legion, before and after the siege of Dien Bien Phu. Some of his stories had the ring of truth, others (particularly his sexual exploits) were obviously tall tales, but I was happy to pay for the beer or coffee in order to hear him spin them out.

Those were glorious days for an unknown freelance writer. I was realizing my dream of living by my pen, and I was doing it from a small town in North India, having turned my back on both London and New Delhi. I had no ambitions to be a great writer, or even a famous one, or even a rich one. All I wanted to do was *write*. And I wanted a few readers and the occasional cheque so I could carry on living my dream.

The cheques came along in their own desultory way—fifty rupees from the *Weekly*, or thirty-five from *The Statesman* or the same from *Sport and Pastime*, and so on—just enough to get by, and to be the envy of Suresh Mathur, William Matheson, and a few others, professional people who felt that I had no business earning more than they did. Suresh even declared that I should have been paying tax and offered to represent me, his other clients having gone elsewhere.

And there was old Colonel Wilkie, living on a small pension in a corner room of the White House Hotel. His wife had left him some years before, presumably because of his drinking, but he claimed to have left her because of her obsession with moving the furniture—it seems she was always shifting things about, changing rooms, throwing out perfectly sound tables and chairs and replacing them with fancy stuff picked up here and there. If he took a liking to a particular easy chair and showed signs of settling down in it, it would disappear the next day to be replaced by something horribly ugly and uncomfortable.

'It was a form of mental torture,' said Colonel Wilkie, confiding in me over a glass of beer on the White House verandah. 'The sitting room was cluttered with all sorts of ornamental junk and flimsy side tables, so that I was constantly falling over the damn things. It was like a minefield! And the mines were never in the same place. You've noticed that I walk with a limp?'

'First World War?' I ventured. 'Wounded at Ypres? Or was it Flanders?'

'Nothing of the sort,' snorted the Colonel. 'I did get one or two flesh wounds but they were nothing as compared to the damage inflicted on me by those damned shifting tables and chairs. Fell over a coffee table and dislocated my shoulder. Then broke an ankle negotiating a stool that was in the wrong place. Bookshelf fell on me. Tripped on a rolled-up carpet. Hit by a curtain rod. Would you have put up with it?'

'No,' I had to admit.

'Had to leave her, of course. She went off to England. Send her an allowance. Half my pension! All spent on furniture!'

'It's a superstition of sorts, I suppose. Collecting things.'

The Colonel told me that the final straw was when his favourite spring bed had suddenly been replaced by a bed made up of hard wooden slats. It was sheer torture trying to sleep on it, and he had left his house and moved into the White House Hotel as a permanent guest.

Now he couldn't allow anyone to touch or tidy up anything in his room. There were beer stains on the tablecloth, cobwebs on his family pictures, dust on his books, empty medicine bottles on his dressing table, and mice nesting in his old, discarded boots. He had gone to the other extreme and wouldn't have anything changed or moved in his room.

I didn't see much of the room because we usually sat out on the verandah, waited upon by one of the hotel bearers, who came over with bottles of beer that I dutifully paid for, the Colonel having exhausted his credit. I suppose he was in his late sixties then. He never went anywhere, not even for a walk in the compound. He blamed this inactivity on his gout, but it was really inertia and an unwillingness to leave the precincts of the bar, where he could cadge the occasional drink from a sympathetic guest. I am that age now, and not half as active as I used to be, but there are people to live for and tales to tell, and I keep writing. It is important to keep writing.

Colonel Wilkie had given up on life. I suppose he could have gone off to England, but he would have been more miserable there, with no one to buy him a drink (since he wasn't likely to reciprocate) and the possibility of his wife turning up again to rearrange the furniture.

3
BIBIJI

My landlady was a remarkable woman, and this little memoir of Dehra in the 1950s would be incomplete without a sketch of hers.

She would often say, 'Ruskin, one day you must write my life story,' and I would promise to do so. And although she really deserves a book to herself, I shall try to do justice to her in these few pages.

She was, in fact, my Punjabi stepfather's first wife. Does that sound confusing? It was certainly complicated. And you might well ask, why on earth were you living with your stepfather's first wife instead of your stepfather and mother?

The answer is simple. I got on rather well with this rotund, well-built lady, and sympathized with her predicament. She had been married at a young age to my stepfather, who was something of a playboy, and who ran the photographic saloon he had received as part of her dowry. When he left her for my mother, he sold the saloon and gave his first wife part of the premises. In order to sustain herself and two small children, she started a small provision store and thus became Dehra's first lady shopkeeper.

I had just started freelancing from Dehra and was not keen on joining my mother and stepfather in Delhi. When 'Bibiji'—as I called her—offered me a portion of her flat on very reasonable terms, I accepted without hesitation and was to spend the next two years above her little shop on Rajpur Road. Almost fifty years later, the flat is still there, but it is now an ice cream parlour! Poetic justice, perhaps.

Bibiji sold the usual provisions. Occasionally, I lent a helping hand and soon learnt the names of the various lentils arrayed before us—*moong, malka, masoor, arhar, channa, rajma*, etc. She bought her rice, flour and other items wholesale from the *mandi*, and sometimes I would accompany her on an early morning march to the mandi (about two miles distant) where we would load a handcart with her purchases. She was immensely strong and could lift sacks of wheat or rice that left me gasping. I can't say I blame my rather skinny stepfather for staying out of her reach.

She had a helper, a Bihari youth, who would trundle the cart back to the shop and help with the loading and unloading. Before opening the shop (at around 8 a.m.) she would make our breakfast—*parathas* with my favourite *shalgam* pickle, and in winter, a delicious *kanji* made from the juice of red carrots. When the shop opened, I would go upstairs to do my writing while she conducted the day's business.

Sometimes she would ask me to help her with her accounts, or in making out a bill, for she was barely literate. But she was an astute shopkeeper; she knew instinctively who was good for credit and who was strictly *nakad* (cash). She would also warn me against friends who borrowed money without any intention of returning it; warnings that I failed to heed. Friends in perpetual need there were aplenty—Sudheer, William, Suresh and a couple of others—and I am amazed that I didn't have to borrow, too, considering the uncertain nature of my income. Those little cheques and money orders from magazines did not always arrive in time. But sooner or later something *did* turn up. I was very lucky.

▪

Bibiji had a friend, a neighbour, Mrs Singh, an attractive woman in her thirties who smoked a hookah and regaled us with tales of ghosts and *chudails* from her village near Agra. We did not see much of her husband who was an excise inspector. He was busy making money.

Bibiji and Mrs Singh were almost inseparable, which was quite understandable in view of the fact that both had absentee husbands. They were really happy together. During the day Mrs Singh would sit in the shop, observing the customers. And afterwards she would entertain us with clever imitations of the more odd or eccentric among them. At night, after the shop was closed, Bibiji and her friend would make themselves comfortable on the same cot (creaking beneath their combined weights), wrap themselves in a *razai* or blanket and invite me to sit on the next *charpai* and listen to their yarns or tell them a few of my own. Mrs Singh had a small son, not very bright, who was continually eating laddoos, jalebis, *barfis* and other sweets. Quite appropriately, he was called Laddoo. And I believe he grew into one.

Bibiji's son and daughter were then at a residential school. They came home occasionally. So did Mr Singh, with more sweets for his son. He did not appear to find anything unusual in his wife's intimate relationship with Bibiji. His mind was obviously on other things.

Bibiji and Mrs Singh both made plans to get me married. When I protested, saying I was only twenty-three, they said I was old enough. Bibiji had an eye on an Anglo-Indian schoolteacher who sometimes came to the shop, but Mrs Singh turned her down, saying she had very spindly legs. Instead, she suggested the daughter of the local padre, a glamorous-looking, dusky beauty, but Bibiji vetoed the proposal, saying the young lady used too much make-up and already displayed too much fat around the waistline. Both agreed that I should marry a plain-looking girl who could cook, use a sewing machine and speak a little English.

'And be strong in the legs,' I added, much to Mrs Singh's approval.

They did not know it, but I was enamoured of Kamla, a girl from the hills, who lived with her parents in quarters behind the flat. She was always giving me mischievous glances with her dark, beautiful, expressive eyes. And whenever I passed her on the landing, we exchanged pleasantries and friendly banter; it was as though we had known each other for a long time. But she was already betrothed, and that too to a much older man, a widower, who owned some land outside the town. Kamla's family was poor, her father was in debt, and it was to be a marriage of convenience. There was nothing much I could do about it—landless and without prospects—but after the marriage had taken place and she had left for her new home, I befriended her younger brother and through him sent her my good wishes from time to time. She is just a distant memory now, but a bright one, like a forget-me-not blooming on a bare rock. Would I have married her, had I been able to? She was simple, unlettered; but I might have taken the chance.

Those two years on Rajpur Road were an eventful time, what with the visitations of Sudheer, the company of William and Suresh, the participation in Bibiji's little shop, the evanescent friendship with Kamla. I did a lot of writing and even sold a few stories here and there; but the returns were modest, barely adequate. Everyone was urging me to try my luck in Delhi. And so I bid goodbye to sleepy little Dehra (as it then was) and took a bus to the capital. I did no better there as a writer, but I found a job of sorts and that kept me going for a couple of years.

But to return to Bibiji, I cannot just leave her in limbo. She continued to run her shop for several years, and it was only failing health that forced her to close it. She sold the business and went to live with her married daughter in New Delhi. I saw her from time to time. In spite of high blood pressure, diabetes and eventually blindness, she lived on into her eighties. She was always glad to see me, and never gave up trying to find a suitable bride for me.

The last time I saw her, shortly before she died, she said, 'Ruskin, there is this widow—lady who lives down the road and comes over sometimes. She has two children but they are grown up. She feels lonely in her big house. If you like, I'll talk to her. It's time you settled down. And she's only sixty.'

'Thanks, Bibiji,' I said, holding both ears. 'But I think I'll settle down in my next life.'

THE LAST TONGA RIDE

It was a warm spring day in Dehra, and the walls of the bungalow were aflame with flowering bougainvillaea. The papayas were ripening. The scent of sweetpeas drifted across the garden. Grandmother sat in an easy chair in a shady corner of the verandah, her knitting needles clicking away, her head nodding now and then. She was knitting a pullover for my father. 'Delhi has cold winters,' she had said, and although the winter was still eight months away, she had set to work on getting our woollens ready.

In the Kathiawar states, touched by the warm waters of the Arabian Sea, it had never been cold but Dehra lies at the foot of the first range of the Himalayas.

Grandmother's hair was white, her eyes were not very strong but her fingers moved quickly with the needles and the needles kept clicking all morning.

When Grandmother wasn't looking, I picked geranium leaves, crushed them between my fingers and pressed them to my nose.

I had been in Dehra with my grandmother for almost a month and I had not seen my father during this time. We had never before been separated for so long. He wrote to me every week, and sent me books and picture postcards; and I would walk to the end of the road to meet the postman as early as possible, to see if there was any mail for us.

We heard the jingle of tonga-bells at the gate, and a familiar horse-buggy came rattling up the drive.

'I'll see who's come,' I said, and ran down the verandah steps and across the garden.

It was Bansi Lal in his tonga. There were many tongas and tonga-drivers in Dehra but Bansi was my favourite driver. He was young and handsome and he always wore a clean white shirt and pyjamas. His pony, too, was bigger and faster than the other tonga ponies. Bansi didn't have a passenger, so I asked him, 'What have you come for, Bansi?'

'Your grandmother sent for me, dost.' He did not call me 'chota sahib' or 'baba', but 'dost' and this made me feel much more important. Not every small boy could boast of a tonga-driver for his friend!

'Where are you going, Granny?' I asked, after I had run back to the verandah.

'I'm going to the bank.'

'Can I come too?'

'Whatever for? What will you do in the bank?'

'Oh, I won't come inside, I'll sit in the tonga with Bansi.'

'Come along, then.'

We helped Grandmother into the back seat of the tonga, and then I joined Bansi in the driver's seat. He said something to his pony, and the pony set off at a brisk trot, out of the gate and down the road.

'Now, not too fast, Bansi,' said Grandmother, who didn't like anything that went too fast—tonga, motor car, train or bullock cart.

'Fast?' said Bansi. 'Have no fear, Memsahib. This pony has never gone fast in its life. Even if a bomb went off behind us, we could go no faster. I have another pony, which I use for racing when customers are in a hurry. This pony is reserved for you, Memsahib.'

There was no other pony, but Grandmother did not know this, and was mollified by the assurance that she was riding in the slowest tonga in Dehra.

A ten-minute ride brought us to the bazaar. Grandmother's bank, the Allahabad Bank, stood near the clock tower. She was gone for about half an hour and during this period Bansi and I sauntered about in front of the shops. The pony had been left with some green stuff to munch.

'Do you have any money on you?' asked Bansi.

'Four annas,' I said.

'Just enough for two cups of tea,' said Bansi, putting his arm round my shoulders and guiding me towards a tea stall. The money passed from my palm to his.

'You can have tea, if you like,' I said. 'I'll have a lemonade.'

'So be it, friend. A tea and a lemonade, and be quick about it,' said Bansi to the boy in the stall and presently the drinks were set before us and Bansi was making a sound rather like his pony when he drank, while I burped my way through some green, gaseous stuff that tasted more like soap than lemonade.

When Grandmother came out of the bank, she looked pensive, and did not talk much during the ride back to the house except to tell me to behave myself when I leaned over to pat the pony on its rump. After paying off Bansi, she marched straight indoors.

'When will you come again?' I asked Bansi.

'When my services are required, dost. I have to make a living, you know. But I tell you what, since we are friends, the next time I am passing this way after leaving a fare, I will jingle my bells at the gate and if you are free and would like a ride—a fast ride—you can join me. It won't cost you anything. Just bring some money for a cup of tea.'

'All right—since we are friends,' I said.

'Since we are friends.'

And touching the pony very lightly with the handle of his whip, he sent the tonga rattling up the drive and out of the gate. I could hear Bansi singing as the pony cantered down the road.

Ayah was waiting for me in the bedroom, her hands resting on her broad hips—sure sign of an approaching storm.

'So you went off to the bazaar without telling me,' she said. (It wasn't enough that I had Grandmother's permission!) 'And all this time I've been waiting to give you your bath.'

'It's too late now, isn't it?' I asked hopefully.

'No, it isn't. There's still an hour left for lunch. Off with your clothes!'

While I undressed, Ayah berated me for keeping the company of tonga-drivers like Bansi. I think she was a little jealous.

'He is a rogue, that man. He drinks, gambles and smokes opium. He has TB and other terrible diseases. So don't you be too friendly with him, understand, baba?'

I nodded my head sagely but said nothing. I thought Ayah was exaggerating, as she always did about people, and besides, I had no intention of giving up free tonga rides.

As my father had told me, Dehra was a good place for trees, and Grandmother's house was surrounded by several kinds—peepul, seem, mango, jackfruit, papaya and an ancient banyan tree. Some of the trees had been planted by my father and grandfather.

'How old is the jackfruit tree?' I asked Grandmother.

'Now let me see,' said Grandmother, looking very thoughtful. 'I should remember the jackfruit tree. Oh yes, your grandfather put it down in 1927. It was during the rainy season. I remember, because it was your father's birthday and we celebrated it by planting a tree. 14 July 1927. Long before you were born!'

The banyan tree grew behind the house. Its spreading branches, which hung to the ground and took root again, formed a number of twisting passageways in which I liked to wander. The tree was older than the house, older than my grandparents, as old as Dehra. I could hide myself in its branches behind thick, green leaves and spy on the world below.

It was an enormous tree, about sixty feet high, and the first time I saw it I trembled with excitement because I had never seen such a marvellous tree before. I approached it slowly, even cautiously, as I wasn't sure the tree wanted my friendship. It looked as though it had many secrets. There were sounds and movement in the branches but I couldn't see who or what made the sounds.

The tree made the first move, the first overture of friendship. It allowed a leaf to fall.

The leaf brushed against my face as it floated down, but before it could reach the ground I caught and held it. I studied the leaf, running my fingers over its smooth, glossy texture. Then I put out my hand and touched the rough bark of the tree and this felt good to me. So I removed my shoes and socks as people do when they enter a holy place; and finding first a foothold and then a handhold on that broad trunk, I pulled myself up with the help of the tree's aerial roots.

As I climbed, it seemed as though someone was helping me; invisible hands, the hands of the spirit in the tree, touched me and helped me climb.

But although the tree wanted me, there were others who were disturbed and alarmed by my arrival. A pair of parrots suddenly shot out of a hole in the trunk and, with shrill cries, flew across the garden—flashes of green and red and gold. A squirrel looked out from behind a branch, saw me, and went scurrying away to inform his friends and relatives.

I climbed higher, looked up, and saw a red beak poised above my head. I shrank away, but the hornbill made no attempt to attack me. He was relaxing in his home, which was a great hole in the tree trunk. Only the bird's head and great beak were showing. He looked at me in a rather bored way, drowsily opening and shutting his eyes.

'So many creatures live here,' I said to myself. 'I hope none of them are dangerous!'

At that moment, the hornbill lunged at a passing cricket. Bill and tree trunk met with a loud and resonant 'Tonk!'

I was so startled that I nearly fell out of the tree. But it was a difficult tree to fall out of! It was full of places where one could sit or even lie down. So I moved away from the hornbill, crawled along a branch that had sent out supports, and so moved quite a distance from the main body of the tree. I left its cold, dark depths for an area penetrated by shafts of sunlight.

No one could see me. I lay flat on the broad branch hidden by a screen of leaves. People passed by on the road below. A sahib in a sun-helmet. His memsahib twirling a coloured silk sun-umbrella. Obviously she did not want to get too brown and be mistaken for a country-born person. Behind them, a pram wheeled along by a nanny.

Then there were a number of Indians; some in white dhotis, some in western clothes, some in loincloths. Some with baskets on their heads. Others with coolies to carry their baskets for them.

A cloud of dust, the blare of a horn, and down the road, like an out-of-condition dragon, came the latest Morris touring car. Then cyclists. Then a man with a basket of papayas balanced on his head. Following him, a man with a performing monkey. This man rattled a little hand drum, and children followed the man and the monkey along the road. They stopped in the shade of a mango tree on the other side of the road. The little red monkey wore a frilled dress and a baby's bonnet. It danced for the children, while the man sang and played his drum.

The clip-clop of a tonga pony, and Bansi's tonga came rattling down the road. I called down to him and he reined in with a shout of surprise, and looked up into the branches of the banyan tree.

'What are you doing up there?' he cried.

'Hiding from Grandmother,' I said.

'And when are you coming for that ride?'

'On Tuesday afternoon,' I said.

'Why not today?'

'Ayah won't let me. But she has Tuesdays off.'

Bansi spat red paan juice across the road. 'Your ayah is jealous,' he said.

'I know,' I said. 'Women are always jealous, aren't they? I suppose it's because she doesn't have a tonga.'

'It's because she doesn't have a tonga-driver,' said Bansi, grinning up at me. 'Never mind. I'll come on Tuesday—that's the day after tomorrow, isn't it?'

I nodded down to him, and then started backing along my branch, because I could hear Ayah calling in the distance. Bansi leant forward and smacked his pony across the rump, and the tonga shot forward.

'What were you doing up there?' asked Ayah a little later.

'I was watching a snake cross the road,' I said. I knew she couldn't resist talking about snakes. There weren't as many in Dehra as there had been in Kathiawar and she was thrilled that I had seen one.

'Was it moving towards you or away from you?' she asked.

'It was going away.'

Ayah's face clouded over. 'That means poverty for the beholder,' she said gloomily.

Later, while scrubbing me down in the bathroom, she began to air all her prejudices, which included drunkards ('they die quickly anyway'), misers ('they get murdered sooner or later') and tonga-drivers ('they have all the vices').

'You are a very lucky boy,' she said suddenly, peering closely at my tummy.

'Why?' I asked. 'You just said I would be poor because I saw a snake going the wrong way.'

'Well, you won't be poor for long. You have a mole on your tummy, and that's very lucky. And there is one under your armpit, which means you will be famous. Do you have one on the neck? No, thank God! A mole on the neck is the sign of a murderer!'

'Do you have any moles?' I asked.

Ayah nodded seriously, and pulling her sleeve up to her shoulder, showed me a large mole high on her arm.

'What does that mean?' I asked.

'It means a life of great sadness,' said Ayah gloomily.

'Can I touch it?' I asked.

'Yes, touch it,' she said, and taking my hand, she placed it against the mole.

'It's a nice mole,' I said, wanting to make Ayah happy. 'Can I kiss it?'

'You can kiss it,' said Ayah.

I kissed her on the mole.

'That's nice,' she said.

Tuesday afternoon came at last, and as soon as Grandmother was asleep and Ayah had gone to the bazaar, I was at the gate, looking up and down the road for Bansi and his tonga. He was not long in coming. Before the tonga turned into the road, I could hear his voice, singing to the accompaniment of the carriage bells. He reached down, took my hand, and hoisted me on to the seat beside him. Then we went off down the road at a steady jogtrot. It was only when we reached the outskirts of the town that Bansi encouraged his pony to greater efforts. He rose in his seat, leaned forward and slapped the pony across the haunches. From a brisk trot we changed to a carefree canter. The tonga swayed from side to side. I clung to Bansi's free arm, while he grinned at me, his mouth red with paan juice.

'Where shall we go, dost?' he asked.

'Nowhere,' I said. 'Anywhere.'

'We'll go to the river,' said Bansi.

The 'river' was really a swift mountain stream that ran through the forests outside Dehra, joining the Ganga about fifteen miles away. It was almost dry during the winter and early summer; in flood during the monsoon.

The road out of Dehra was a gentle decline and soon we were rushing headlong through the tea gardens and eucalyptus forests, the pony's hoofs striking sparks off the metalled road, the carriage wheels groaning and creaking so loudly that I feared one of them would come off and that we would all be thrown into a ditch or into the small canal that ran beside the road. We swept through mango groves, through guava and litchi orchards, past broad-leaved sal and shisham trees. Once in the sal forest, Bansi turned the tonga on to a rough cart track, and we continued along it for about a furlong, until the road dipped down to the stream bed.

'Let us go straight into the water,' said Bansi. 'You and I and the pony!' And he drove the tonga straight into the middle of the stream, where the water came up to the pony's knees.

'I am not a great one for baths,' said Bansi, 'but the pony needs one, and why should a horse smell sweeter than its owner?' Saying which, he flung off his clothes and jumped into the water.

'Better than bathing under a tap!' he cried, slapping himself on the chest and thighs. 'Come down, dost, and join me!'

After some hesitation I joined him, but had some difficulty in keeping on my feet in the fast current. I grabbed at the pony's tail, and hung on to it, while Bansi began sloshing water over the patient animal's back.

After this, Bansi led both me and the pony out of the stream and together we gave the carriage a good washing down. I'd had a free ride and Bansi got the services of a free helper for the long overdue spring cleaning of his tonga. After we had finished the job, he presented me with a packet of aam papar—a sticky toffee made from mango pulp—and for some time I tore at it as a dog tears at a hit of old leather. Then I felt drowsy and lay down on the brown, sun-warmed grass. Crickets and grasshoppers were telephoning each other from tree and bush and a pair of bluejays rolled, dived and swooped acrobatically overhead.

Bansi had no watch. He looked at the sun and said, 'It is past three. When will that ayah of yours be home? She is more frightening than your grandmother!'

'She comes at four.'

'Then we must hurry back. And don't tell her where we've been, or I'll never be able to come to your house again. Your grandmother's one of my best customers.'

'That means you'd be sorry if she died.'

'I would indeed, my friend.'

Bansi raced the tonga back to town. There was very little motor traffic in those days, and tongas and bullock carts were far more numerous than they are today.

We were back five minutes before Ayah returned. Before Bansi left, he promised to take me for another ride the following week.

The house in Dehra had to be sold. My father had not left any money; he had never realized that his health would deteriorate so rapidly from the malarial fevers, which had grown in frequency. He was still planning for the future when he died. Now that my father had gone, Grandmother saw no point in staying on in India; there was nothing left in the bank and she needed money for our passages to England, so the house had to go. Dr Ghose, who had a thriving medical practice in Dehra, made her a reasonable offer, which she accepted.

Then things happened very quickly. Grandmother sold most of our belongings, because as she said, we wouldn't be able to cope with a lot of luggage. The *kabaris* came in droves, buying our crockery, furniture, carpets and clocks at throwaway prices. Grandmother hated parting with some of her possessions, such as the carved giltwood mirror, her walnut-wood armchair and her rosewood writing desk, but it was impossible to take them with us. They were carried away in a bullock cart.

Ayah was very unhappy at first but cheered up when Grandmother got her a job with a tea-planter's family in Assam. It was arranged that she could stay with us until we left Dehra.

We left at the end of September, just as the monsoon clouds broke up, scattered, and were driven away by soft breezes from the Himalayas. There was no time to revisit the island where my father and I had planted our trees. And in the urgency and excitement of the preparations for our departure, I forgot to recover my small treasures from the hole in the banyan tree. It was only when we were in Bansi's tonga, on the way to the station, that I remembered my top, catapult and Iron Cross. Too late! To go back for them would mean missing the train.

'Hurry!' urged Grandmother nervously. 'We mustn't be late for the train, Bansi.'

Bansi flicked the reins and shouted to his pony, and for

once in her life Grandmother submitted to being carried along the road at a brisk trot.

'It's five to nine,' she said, 'and the train leaves at nine.'

'Do not worry, Memsahib. I have been taking you to the station for fifteen years, and you have never missed a train!'

'No,' said Grandmother. 'And I don't suppose you'll ever take me to the station again, Bansi.'

'Times are changing, Memsahib. Do you know that there is now a taxi—a *motor car*—competing with the tongas of Dehra? You are lucky to be leaving. If you stay, you will see me starve to death!'

'We will all starve to death if we don't catch that train,' said Grandmother.

'Do not worry about the train, it never leaves on time, and no one expects it to. If it left at nine o' clock, everyone would miss it.'

Bansi was right. We arrived at the station at five minutes past nine, and rushed on to the platform, only to find that the train had not yet arrived.

The platform was crowded with people waiting to catch the same train or to meet people arriving on it. Ayah was there already, standing guard over a pile of miscellaneous luggage. We sat down on our boxes and became part of the platform life at an Indian railway station.

Moving among piles of bedding and luggage were sweating, cursing coolies; vendors of magazines, sweetmeats, tea and betel-leaf preparations; also stray dogs, stray people and sometimes a stray stationmaster. The cries of the vendors mixed with the general clamour of the station and the shunting of a steam engine in the yards. 'Tea, hot tea!' Sweets, papads, hot stuff, cold drinks, toothpowder, pictures of film stars, bananas, balloons, wooden toys, clay images of the gods. The platform had become a bazaar.

Ayah was giving me all sorts of warnings.

'Remember, baba, don't lean out of the window when the train is moving. There was that American boy who lost his head last year! And don't eat rubbish at every station between here and Bombay. And see that no strangers enter the compartment. Mr Wilkins was murdered *and* robbed last year!'

The station bell clanged, and in the distance there appeared a big, puffing steam engine, painted green and gold and black. A stray dog, with a lifetime's experience of trains, darted away across the railway lines. As the train came alongside the platform, doors opened, window shutters fell, faces appeared in the openings, and even before the train had come to a stop, people were trying to get in or out.

For a few moments there was chaos. The crowd surged backward and forward. No one could get out. No one could get in. A hundred people were leaving the train, two hundred were getting into it. No one wanted to give way.

The problem was solved by a man climbing out of a window. Others followed his example and the pressure at the doors eased and people started squeezing into their compartments.

Grandmother had taken the precaution of reserving berths in a first-class compartment, and assisted by Bansi and half a dozen coolies, we were soon inside with all our luggage. A whistle blasted and we were off! Bansi had to jump from the running train.

As the engine gathered speed, I ignored Ayah's advice and put my head out of the window to look back at the receding platform. Ayah and Bansi were standing on the platform, waving to me and I kept waving to them until the train rushed into the darkness and the bright lights of Dehra were swallowed up in the night. New lights, dim and flickering came into existence as we passed small villages. The stars too were visible and I saw a shooting star streaking through the heavens.

I remembered something that Ayah had once told me, that stars are the spirits of good men, and I wondered if that shooting star was a sign from my father that he was aware of our departure and would be with us on our journey. And I remembered something else that Ayah had said—that if one wished on a shooting star, one's wish would be granted, provided of course that one thrust all five fingers into the mouth at the same time!

'What on earth are you doing?' asked Grandmother staring at me as I thrust my hand into my mouth.

'Making a wish,' I said.

'Oh,' said Grandmother.

She was preoccupied, and didn't ask me what I was wishing for; nor did I tell her.

'LET'S GO TO THE PICTURES!'

My love affair with the cinema began when I was five and ended when I was about fifty. Not because I wanted it to, but because all my favourite cinema halls were closing down—being turned into shopping malls or garages or just disappearing altogether.

There was something magical about sitting in a darkened cinema hall, the audience silent, completely focussed on the drama unfolding on the big screen. You could escape to a different world—run away to Dover with David Copperfield, sail away to a treasure island with Long John Silver, dance the light fantastic with Fred Astaire or Gene Kelly, sing with Saigal or Deanna Durbin or Nelson Eddy, fall in love with Madhubala or Elizabeth Taylor. And until the lights came on at the end of the show you were in their world, far removed from the troubles of one's own childhood or the struggles of early manhood.

Watching films on TV cannot be the same. People come and go, the power comes and goes, other viewers keep switching the channels, food is continually being served or consumed, family squabbles are ever present, and there is no escape from those dreaded commercials that are repeated every ten or fifteen minutes, or even between overs if you happen to be watching cricket.

No longer do we hear that evocative suggestion: 'Let's go to the pictures!'

Living in Mussoorie where there are no longer any functioning cinemas, the invitation is heard no more. I'm afraid there isn't half as much excitement in the words 'Let's put on the TV!'

For one thing, going to the pictures meant going out—on foot, or on a bicycle, or in the family car. When I lived on the outskirts of Mussoorie it took me almost an hour to climb the hill into town to see a film at one of our tiny halls—but walk I did, in hot sun or drenching rain or icy wind, because going to the pictures was an event in itself, a break from more mundane activities, quite often a social occasion. You would meet friends from other parts of the town, and after the show you would join them in a cafe for a cup of tea and the latest gossip. A stroll along the Mall and a visit to the local bookshop would bring the evening to a satisfying end. A long walk home under the stars, a drink before dinner, something to listen to on the radio... 'And then to bed,' as Mr Pepys would have said.

Not that everything went smoothly in our small-town cinemas. In Shimla, Mussoorie and other hill stations, the roofs were of corrugated tin sheets, and when there was heavy rain or a hailstorm it would be impossible to hear the soundtrack. You had then to imagine that you were back in the silent film era.

Mussoorie's oldest cinema, the Picture Palace, did in fact open early in the silent era. This was in 1912, the year electricity came to the town. Later, its basement floor was also turned into a cinema, the Jubilee, which probably made it India's first multiplex hall. Sadly, both closed down about five years ago, along with the Rialto, the Majestic and the Capitol (below Halman's Hotel).

In Shimla, we had the Ritz, the Regal and the Rivoli. This was when I was a schoolboy at Bishop Cotton's. How we used to look forward to our summer and autumn breaks. We would be allowed into town during these holidays, and we lost no time in tramping up to the Ridge to take in the latest films. Sometimes we'd arrive wet or perspiring, but the changeable weather did not prevent us from enjoying the film. One-and-a-half hours escape from the routine and discipline of boarding school life. Fast foods had yet to be invented, but roasted peanuts or *bhuttas* would keep us going. They were cheap too. The cinema ticket was just over a rupee. If you had five rupees in your pocket you could enjoy a pleasant few hours in the town.

It was during the winter holidays—three months of time on my hands—that I really caught up with the films of the day.

New Delhi, the winter of 1943. Second World War was still in progress. The halls were flooded with British and American movies. My father would return from Air Headquarters, where he'd been working on cyphers all day. 'Let's go to the pictures,' he'd say, and we'd be off to the Regal or Rivoli or Odeon or Plaza, only a short walk from our rooms on Atul Grove Road.

Comedies were my favourites. Laurel and Hardy, Abbot and Costello, George Formby, Harold Lloyd, the Marx Brothers... And sometimes we'd venture further afield, to the old Ritz at Kashmere Gate, to see Sabu in *The Thief of Baghdad* or *Cobra Woman.* These *Arabian Nights*-type entertainments were popular in the old city.

The Statesman, the premier newspaper of that era, ran ads for all the films in town, and I'd cut them out and stick them in a scrapbook. I could rattle off the cast of all the pictures I'd seen, and today, sixty years later, I can still name all the actors (and sometimes the director) of almost every 1940s film.

My father died when I was ten and I went to live with my mother and stepfather in Dehradun. Dehra too, was well served with cinemas, but I was a lonely picturegoer. I had no friends or companions in those years, and I would trudge off on my own to the Orient or Odeon or Hollywood, to indulge in a few hours of escapism. Books were there, of course, providing another and better form of escape, but books had to be read in the home, and sometimes I wanted to get away from the house and pursue a solitary other-life in the anonymous privacy of a darkened cinema hall.

It has gone now, the little Odeon cinema opposite the old Parade Ground in Dehra. Many of my age, and younger, will remember it with affection, for it was probably the most popular meeting place for English cinema buffs in the '40s and '50s. You could get a good idea of the popularity of a film by looking at the number of bicycles ranged outside. Dehra was a bicycle town. The scooter hadn't been invented, and cars were few. I belonged to a minority of walkers. I have walked all over the towns and cities I have lived in—Dehradun, New and Old Delhi, London, St Helier (in Jersey) and our hill stations. Those walks often ended at the cinema!

The Odeon was a twenty-minute walk from the Old Survey Road, where we lived at the time, and after the evening show I would walk home across the deserted parade ground, the starry night adding to my dreams of a starry world, where tap dancers, singing cowboys, swashbuckling swordsmen and glamorous women in *sarongs* reigned supreme in the firmament. I wasn't just a daydreamer; I was a star-dreamer.

During the intervals (five-minute breaks between the shorts and the main feature), the projectionist or his assistant would play a couple of gramophone records for the benefit of the audience. Unfortunately, the management had only two or three records, and the audience would grow restless listening to the same tunes at every show. I must have been compelled to listen to 'Don't Fence Me In' about a hundred times, and felt thoroughly fenced in.

At home, I had a good collection of gramophone records, passed on to me by relatives and neighbours who were leaving India around the time of Independence. I decided it would be a good idea to give some of them to the cinema's management so that we could be provided with a little more variety during the intervals. I made a selection of about twenty records—mostly dance music of the period—and presented them to the manager, Mr Suri.

Mr Suri was delighted. And to show me his gratitude, he presented me with a Free Pass which permitted me to see all the pictures I liked without having to buy a ticket! Any day, any show, for as long as Mr Suri was the manager! Could any ardent picturegoer have asked for more?

This unexpected bonanza lasted for almost two years with the result that during my school holidays I saw a film every second day. Two days was the average run for most films. Except *Gone With the Wind,* which ran for a week, to my great chagrin. I found it so boring that I left in the middle.

Usually I did enjoy films based on famous or familiar books. Dickens was a natural for the screen. *David Copperfield, Oliver Twist, Great Expectations, Nicholas Nickleby, A Tale of Two Cities, Pickwick Papers, A Christmas Carol* all made successful films, true to the originals. Daphne du Maurier's novels also transferred well to the screen. As did Somerset Maugham's works: *Of Human Bondage, The Razor's Edge, The Letter, Rain* and several others.

Occasionally I brought the management a change of records. Mr Suri was not a very communicative man, but I think he liked me (he knew something about my circumstances) and with a smile and a wave of the hand he would indicate that the freedom of the hall was mine.

Eventually, school finished, I was packed off to England, where my picture-going days went into a slight decline. No

Free Passes any more. But on Jersey island, where I lived and worked for a year, I found an out-of-the-way cinema which specialized in showing old comedies, and here I caught up with many British film comedians such as Tommy Trinder, Sidney Howard, Max Miller, Will Hay, Old Mother Riley (a man in reality) and Gracie Fields. These artistes had been but names to me, as their films had never come to India. I was thrilled to be able to discover and enjoy their considerable talents. You would be hard put to find their films today; they have seldom been revived.

In London for two years I had an office job and most of my spare time was spent in writing (and rewriting) my first novel. All the same, I took to the streets and discovered the Everyman cinema in Hampstead, which showed old classics, including the films of Jean Renoir and Orson Welles. And the Academy in Leicester Square, which showed the best films from the continent. I also discovered a couple of seedy little cinemas in the East End, which appropriately showed the early gangster films of James Cagney and Humphrey Bogart.

I also saw the first Indian film to get a regular screening in London. It was called *Aan,* and was the usual extravagant mix of music and melodrama. But it ran for two or three weeks. Homesick Indians (which included me) flocked to see it. One of its stars was Nadira, who specialized in playing the scheming sultry villainess. A few years ago she came out of retirement to take the part of Miss Mackenzie in a TV serial based on some of my short stories set in Mussoorie. A sympathetic role for a change. And she played it to perfection.

It was four years before I saw Dehra again. Mr Suri had gone elsewhere. The little cinema had closed down and was about to be demolished, to make way for a hotel and a block of shops.

We must move on, of course. There's no point in hankering

after distant pleasures and lost picture palaces. But there's no harm in indulging in a little nostalgia. What is nostalgia, after all, but an attempt to preserve that which was good in the past?

And last year I was reminded of that golden era of the silver screen. I was rummaging around in a kabari shop in one of Dehradun's bazaars where I came across a pile of old 78 RPM records, all looking a little the worse for wear. And on a couple of them I found my name scratched on the labels. 'Pennies from Heaven' was the title of one of the songs. It had certainly saved me a few rupees. That and the goodwill of Mr Suri, the Odeon's manager, all those years ago.

I bought the records. Can't play them now. No wind-up gramophone! But I am a sentimental fellow and I keep them among my souvenirs as a reminder of the days when I walked home alone across the silent, moonlit parade ground, after the evening show was over.

BE PREPARED

I was a Boy Scout once, although I couldn't tell a slip knot from a granny knot, nor a reef knot from a thief knot. I did know that a thief knot was to be used to tie up a thief, should you happen to catch one. I have never caught a thief—and wouldn't know what to do with one since I can't tie the right knot. I'd just let him go with a warning, I suppose. And tell him to become a Boy Scout.

'Be prepared!' That's the Boy Scout motto. And it is a good one, too. But I never seem to be well prepared for anything, be it an exam or a journey or the roof blowing off my room. I get halfway through a speech and then forget what I have to say next. Or I make a new suit to attend a friend's wedding, and then turn up in my pyjamas.

So, how did I, the most impractical of boys, survive as a Boy Scout?

Well, it seems a rumour had gone around the junior school (I was still a junior then) that I was a good cook. I had never cooked anything in my life, but of course I had spent a lot of time in the tuck shop making suggestions and advising Chimpu, who ran the tuck shop, and encouraging him to make more and better samosas, jalebis, tikkees and pakoras. For my unwanted advice, he would favour me with an occasional free samosa. So, naturally, I looked upon him as a friend and benefactor. With this qualification, I was given a cookery badge and put in charge of our troop's supply of rations.

There were about twenty of us in our troop. During the summer break our Scoutmaster, Mr Oliver, took us on a camping expedition to Taradevi, a temple-crowned mountain a few miles outside Shimla. That first night we were put to work, peeling potatoes, skinning onions, shelling peas and pounding masalas. These various ingredients being ready, I was asked, as the troop cookery expert, what should be done with them.

'Put everything in that big *degchi*,' I ordered. 'Pour half a tin of ghee over the lot. Add some nettle leaves, and cook for half an hour.'

When this was done, everyone had a taste, but the general opinion was that the dish lacked something. 'More salt,' I suggested.

More salt was added. It still lacked something. 'Add a cup of sugar,' I ordered.

Sugar was added to the concoction, but it still lacked something.

'We forgot to add tomatoes,' said one of the Scouts. 'Never mind,' I said. 'We have tomato sauce. Add a bottle of tomato sauce!'

'How about some vinegar?' suggested another boy. 'Just the thing,' I said. 'Add a cup of vinegar!'

'Now it's too sour,' said one of the tasters.

'What jam did we bring?' I asked.

'Gooseberry jam.'

'Just the thing. Empty the bottle!'

The dish was a great success. Everyone enjoyed it, including Mr Oliver, who had no idea what had gone into it.

'What's this called?' he asked.

'It's an all-Indian sweet-and-sour jam-potato curry,' I ventured.

'For short, just call it Bond bhujjia,' said one of the boys. I had earned my cookery badge!

Poor Mr Oliver; he wasn't really cut out to be a Scoutmaster, any more than I was meant to be a Scout.

The following day, he told us he would give us a lesson in tracking. Taking a half-hour start, he walked into the forest, leaving behind him a trail of broken twigs, chicken feathers, pine cones and chestnuts. We were to follow the trail until we found him.

Unfortunately, we were not very good trackers. We did follow Mr Oliver's trail some way into the forest, but then we were distracted by a pool of clear water. It looked very inviting. Abandoning our uniforms, we jumped into the pool and had a great time romping about or just lying on its grassy banks and enjoying the sunshine. Many hours later, feeling hungry, we returned to our campsite and set about preparing the evening meal. It was Bond bhujjia again, but with a few variations.

It was growing dark, and we were beginning to worry about Mr Oliver's whereabouts when he limped into the camp, assisted by a couple of local villagers. Having waited for us at the far end of the forest for a couple of hours, he had decided to return by following his own trail, but in the gathering gloom he was soon lost. Village folk returning home from the temple took charge and escorted him back to the camp. He was very angry and made us return all our good-conduct and other badges, which he stuffed into his haversack. I had to give up my cookery badge.

An hour later, when we were all preparing to get into our sleeping bags for the night, Mr Oliver called out, 'Where's dinner?'

'We've had ours,' said one of the boys. 'Everything is finished, sir.'

'Where's Bond? He's supposed to be the cook. Bond, get up and make me an omelette.'

'I can't, sir.'

'Why not?'

'You have my badge. Not allowed to cook without it. Scout rule, sir.'

'I've never heard of such a rule. But you can take your badges, all of you. We return to school tomorrow.'

Mr Oliver returned to his tent in a huff.

But I relented and made him a grand omelette, garnishing it with dandelion leaves and a chilli.

'Never had such an omelette before,' confessed Mr Oliver.

'Would you like another, sir?'

'Tomorrow, Bond, tomorrow. We'll breakfast early tomorrow.'

But we had to break up our camp before we could do that because in the early hours of the next morning, a bear strayed into our camp, entered the tent where our stores were kept, and created havoc with all our provisions, even rolling our biggest degchi down the hillside.

In the confusion and uproar that followed, the bear entered Mr Oliver's tent (our Scoutmaster was already outside, fortunately) and came out entangled in his dressing gown. It then made off towards the forest, a comical sight in its borrowed clothes.

And though we were a troop of brave little scouts, we thought it better to let the bear keep the gown.

ADVENTURES IN READING

1

You don't see them so often now, those tiny books and almanacs—genuine pocket books—once so popular with our parents and grandparents; much smaller than the average paperback, often smaller than the palm of the hand. With the advent of coffee-table books, new books keep growing bigger and bigger, rivalling tombstones! And one day, like Alice after drinking from the wrong bottle, they will reach the ceiling and won't have anywhere else to go. The average publisher, who apparently believes that large profits are linked to large books, must look upon these old miniatures with amusement or scorn. They were not meant for a coffee table, true. They were meant for true book lovers and readers, for they took up very little space—you could slip them into your pocket without any discomfort, either to you or to the pocket.

I have a small collection of these little books, treasured over the years. Foremost is my father's prayer book and psalter, with his name, 'Aubrey Bond, Lovedale, 1917', inscribed on the inside back cover. Lovedale is a school in the Nilgiri Hills in South India, where, as a young man, he did his teacher's training. He gave it to me soon after I went to a boarding school in Shimla in 1944, and my own name is inscribed on it in his beautiful handwriting.

Another beautiful little prayer book in my collection is called *The Finger Prayer Book*. Bound in soft leather, it is about the same length and breadth as the average middle finger. Replete with psalms, it is the complete book of common prayer and not an abridgement; a marvel of miniature book production.

Not much larger is a delicate item in calf leather, *The Humour of Charles Lamb*. It fits into my wallet and often stays there. It has a tiny portrait of the great essayist, followed by some thirty to forty extracts from his essays, such as this favourite of mine: 'Every dead man must take upon himself to be lecturing me with his odious truism, that "Such as he is now, I must shortly be". Not so shortly, friend, perhaps as thou imaginest. In the meantime, I am alive. I move about. I am worth twenty of thee. Know thy betters!'

No fatalist, Lamb. He made no compromise with Father Time. He affirmed that in age, we must be as glowing and tempestuous as in youth! And yet Lamb is thought to be an old-fashioned writer.

Another favourite among my 'little' books is *The Pocket Trivet: An Anthology for Optimists*, published by *The Morning Post* newspaper in 1932. But what is a trivet? the unenlightened may well ask. Well, it's a stand for a small pot or kettle, fixed securely over a grate. To be right as a trivet is to be perfectly right. Just right, like the short sayings in this book, which are further enlivened by a number of charming woodcuts based on the seventeenth century originals, such as the illustration of a moth hovering over a candle flame and below it the legend—'I seeke mine owne hurt.'

But the sayings are mostly of a cheering nature, such as Emerson's 'Hitch your wagon to a star' or the West Indian proverb: 'Every day no Christmas, an' every day no rainy day.'

My book of trivets is a happy example of much concentrated wisdom being collected in a small space—the beauty separated from the dross. It helps me to forget the dilapidated building in which I live and to look instead at the ever-changing cloud patterns as seen from my bedroom windows. There is no end to the shapes made by the clouds, or to the stories they set off in my head. We don't have to circle the world in order to find beauty and fulfilment. After all, most of living has to happen in the mind. And, to quote one anonymous sage from my trivet, 'The world is only the size of each man's head.'

2

Amongst the current fraternity of writers, I must be that very rare person—an author who actually writes by hand!

Soon after the invention of the typewriter, most editors and publishers understandably refused to look at any mansucript that was handwritten. A decade or two earlier, when Dickens and Balzac had submitted their hefty manuscrips in longhand, no one had raised any objection. Had their handwriting been awful, their manuscripts would still have been read. Fortunately for all concerned, most writers, famous or obscure, took pains over their handwriting. For some, it was an art in itself, and many of those early manuscripts are a pleasure to look at and read.

And it wasn't only authors who wrote with an elegant hand. Parents and grandparents of most of us had distinctive styles of their own. I still have my father's last letter, written to me when I was at boarding school in Shimla some fifty years ago. He used large, beautifully formed letters, and his thoughts seemed to have the same flow and clarity as his handwriting.

In his letter he advises me (then a nine-year-old) about my own handwriting: 'I wanted to write before about your writing.

Ruskin... Sometimes I get letters from you in very small writing, as if you wanted to squeeze everything into one sheet of letter paper. It is not good for you or for your eyes, to get into the habit of writing too small... Try and form a larger style of handwriting—use more paper if necessary!'

I did my best to follow his advice, and I'm glad to report that after nearly forty years of the writing life, most people can still read my handwriting!

Word processors are all the rage now, and I have no objection to these mechanical aids any more than I have to my old Olympia typewriter, made in 1956 and still going strong. Although I do all my writing in longhand, I follow the conventions by typing a second draft. But I would not enjoy my writing if I had to do it straight on to a machine. It isn't just the pleasure of writing longhand. I like taking my notebooks and writing pads to odd places. This particular essay is being written on the steps of my small cottage facing Pari Tibba (Fairy Hill). Part of the reason for sitting here is that there is a new postman on this route, and I don't want him to miss me.

For a freelance writer, the postman is almost as important as a publisher. I could, of course, sit here doing nothing, but as I have pencil and paper with me, and feel like using them, I shall write until the postman comes and maybe after he has gone, too! There is really no way in which I could set up a word processor on these steps.

There are a number of favourite places where I do my writing. One is under the chestnut tree on the slope above the cottage. Word processors were not designed keeping mountain slopes in mind. But armed with a pen (or pencil) and paper, I can lie on the grass and write for hours. On one occasion last month, I did take my typewriter into the garden, and I am still trying to extricate an acorn from under the keys, while the roller seems permanently stained yellow with some fine pollen dust from the deodar trees.

My friends keep telling me about all the wonderful things I can do with a word processor, but they haven't got around to finding me one that I can take to bed, for that is another place where I do much of my writing—especially on cold winter nights, when it is impossible to keep the cottage warm.

While the wind howls outside, and snow piles up on the windowsill, I am warm under my quilt, writing pad on my knees, ballpoint pen at the ready. And if, next day, the weather is warm and sunny, these simple aids will accompany me on a long walk, ready for instant use should I wish to record an incident, a prospect, a conversation, or simply a train of thought.

When I think of the great eighteenth- and nineteenth-century writers, scratching away with their quill pens, filling hundreds of pages every month, I am amazed to find that their handwriting did not deteriorate into the sort of hieroglyphics that often make up the average doctor's prescription today. They knew they had to write legibly, if only for the sake of the typesetters.

Both Dickens and Thackeray had good, clear, flourishing styles. (Thackeray was a clever illustrator, too.) Somerset Maugham had an upright, legible hand. Churchill's neat handwriting never wavered, even when he was under stress. I like the bold, clear, straightforward hand of Abraham Lincoln; it mirrors the man. Mahatma Gandhi, another great soul who fell to the assassin's bullet, had many similarities of both handwriting and outlook.

Not everyone had a beautiful hand. King Henry VIII had an untidy scrawl, but then, he was not a man of much refinement. Guy Fawkes, who tried to blow up the British Parliament, had a very shaky hand. With such a quiver, no wonder he failed in his attempt! Hitler's signature is ugly, as you would expect.

And Napoleon's doesn't seem to know where to stop; how much like the man!

I think my father was right when he said handwriting was often the key to a man's character, and that large, well-formed letters went with an uncluttered mind. Florence Nightingale had a lovely handwriting, the hand of a caring person. And there were many like her amongst our forebears.

3

When I was a small boy, no Christmas was really complete unless my Christmas stocking contained several recent issues of my favourite comic paper. If today my friends complain that I am too voracious a reader of books, they have only these comics to blame, for they were the origin, if not of my tastes in reading, then certainly of the reading habit itself.

I like to think that my conversion to comics began at the age of five, with a comic strip on the children's page of *The Statesman*. In the late 1930s, Benji, whose head later appeared only on the Benji League badge, had a strip to himself; I don't remember his adventures very clearly, but every day (or was it once a week?), I would cut out the Benji strip and paste it into a scrapbook. Two years later, this scrapbook, bursting with the adventures of Benji, accompanied me to boarding school, where, of course, it passed through several hands before finally passing into limbo.

Of course, comics did not form the only reading matter that found its way into my Christmas stocking. Before I was eight, I had read *Peter Pan, Alice's Adventures in Wonderland,* and most of *Mr Midshipman Easy*; but I had also consumed thousands of comic papers which were, after all, slim affairs and mostly pictorial, 'certain little penny books radiant with gold and rich with bad pictures', as Leigh Hunt described the children's papers of his own time.

But though they were mostly pictorial, comics in those days did have a fair amount of reading matter, too. *The Hotspur, The Wizard, The Magnet* (a victim of the Second World War) and *The Champion* contained stories woven round certain popular characters. In *The Champion*, which I read regularly right through my prep school years, there was Rockfist Rogan, Royal Air Force (R.A.F.), a pugilist who managed to combine boxing with bombing, and Fireworks Flynn, a footballer who always scored the winning goal in the last two minutes of play.

Billy Bunter has, of course, become one of the immortals—almost a subject for literary and social historians. Quite recently, *The Times Literary Supplement* devoted its first two pages to an analysis of the Bunter stories. Eminent lawyers and doctors still look back nostalgically to the arrival of the weekly *Magnet*; they are now the principal customers for the special souvenir edition of the first issue of the *Magnet*, recently reprinted in facsimile. Bunter, 'forever young', has become a folk hero. He is seen on stage, screen and television, and is even quoted in the House of Commons.

From this, I take courage. My only regret is that I did not preserve my own early comics—not because of any bibliophilic value which they might possess today, but because of my sentimental regard for early influences in art and literature.

The first venture in children's publishing, in 1774, was a comic of sorts. In that year, John Newberry brought out:

> According to Act of Parliament (neatly bound and gilt): *A Little Pretty Pocket-Book, intended for the Amusement of Little Master Tommy and Pretty Miss Polly with Two Letters from Jack the Giant Killer.*

The book contained pictures, rhymes and games. Newberry's characters and imaginary authors included Woglog the Great

Giant, Tommy Trip, Giles Gingerbread, Nurse Truelove, Peregrine Puzzlebrains, Primrose Prettyface, and many others with names similar to those found in the comic papers of our own century.

Newberry was also the originator of the 'Amazing Free Offer', so much a part of American comics. At the beginning of 1755, he had this to offer:

> *Nurse Truelove's New Year Gift, or the Book of Books for Children,* adorned with Cuts and designed as a Present for every little boy who would become a great Man and ride upon a fine Horse; and to every little Girl who would become a great Woman and ride in a Lord Mayor's gilt Coach. Printed for the Author, who has ordered these books to be given gratis to all little Boys in St. Paul's churchyard, they paying for the Binding, which is only Two pence each Book.

Many of today's comics are crude and, like many television serials, violent in their appeal. But I did not know American comics until I was twelve, and by then, I had become quite discriminating. Superman, Bulletman, Batman and Green Lantern, and other super heroes all left me cold. I had, by then, passed into the world of real books but the weakness for the comic strip remains. I no longer receive comics in my Christmas stocking, but I do place a few in the stockings of Gautam and Siddharth. And, needless to say, I read them right through beforehand.

THE ROOM OF MANY COLOURS

Last week I wrote a story, and all the time I was writing it I thought it was a good story; but when it was finished and I had read it through, I found that there was something missing, that it didn't ring true. So I tore it up. I wrote a poem about an old man sleeping in the sun, and this was true, but it was finished quickly, and once again I was left with the problem of what to write next. And I remembered my father, who taught me to write, and I thought, why not write about my father, and about the trees we planted, and about the people I knew while growing up and about what happened on the way to growing up...

And so, like Alice, I must begin at the beginning. In the beginning there was this red insect, just like a velvet button, which I found on the front lawn of the bungalow. The grass was still wet with overnight rain.

I placed the insect on the palm of my hand and took it into the house to show my father.

'Look, Dad,' I said, 'I haven't seen an insect like this before. Where has it come from?'

'Where did you find it?' he asked.

'On the grass.'

'It must have come down from the sky,' he said. 'It must have come down with the rain.'

Later he told me how the insect really happened but I

preferred his first explanation. It was more fun to have it dropping from the sky.

I was seven at the time, and my father was thirty-seven, but, right from the beginning, he made me feel that I was old enough to talk to him about everything—insects, people, trees, steam engines, King George, comics, crocodiles, the Mahatma, the Viceroy, America, Mozambique and Timbuctoo. We took long walks together, explored old ruins, chased butterflies and waved to passing trains.

My mother had gone away when I was four, and I had very dim memories of her. Most other children had their mothers with them, and I found it a bit strange that mine couldn't stay. Whenever I asked my father why she'd gone, he'd say, 'You'll understand when you grow up.' And if I asked him *where* she had gone, he'd look troubled and say, 'I really don't know.' This was the only question of mine to which he didn't have an answer.

But I was quite happy living alone with my father; I had never known any other kind of life.

We were sitting on an old wall, looking out to sea at a couple of Arab dhows and a tram steamer, when my father said, 'Would you like to go to sea one day?'

'Where does the sea go?' I asked.

'It goes everywhere.'

'Does it go to the end of the world?'

'It goes right round the world. It's a round world.'

'It can't be.'

'It is. But it's so big, you can't see the roundness. When a fly sits on a watermelon, it can't see right round the melon, can it? The melon must seem quite flat to the fly. Well, in comparison to the world, we're much, much smaller than the tiniest of insects.'

'Have you been around the world?' I asked.

'No, only as far as England. That's where your grandfather was born.'

'And my grandmother?'

'She came to India from Norway when she was quite small. Norway is a cold land, with mountains and snow, and the sea cutting deep into the land. I was there as a boy. It's very beautiful, and the people are good and work hard.'

'I'd like to go there.'

'You will, one day. When you are older, I'll take you to Norway.'

'Is it better than England?'

'It's quite different.'

'Is it better than India?'

'It's quite different.'

'Is India like England?'

'No, it's different.'

'Well, what does "different" mean?'

'It means things are not the same. It means people are different. It means the weather is different. It means trees and birds and insects are different.'

'Are English crocodiles different from Indian crocodiles?'

'They don't have crocodiles in England.'

'Oh, then it must be different.'

'It would be a dull world if it was the same everywhere,' said my father.

He never lost patience with my endless questioning. If he wanted a rest, he would take out his pipe and spend a long time lighting it. If this took very long I'd find something else to do. But sometimes I'd wait patiently until the pipe was drawing, and then return to the attack.

'Will we always be in India?' I asked.

'No, we'll have to go away one day. You see, it's hard to

explain, but it isn't really our country.'

'Ayah says it belongs to the king of England, and the jewels in his crown were taken from India, and that when the Indians get their jewels back the king will lose India! But first they have to get the crown from the king, but this is very difficult, she says, because the crown is always on his head. He even sleeps wearing his crown!'

Ayah was my nanny. She loved me deeply, and was always filling my head with strange and wonderful stories.

My father did not comment on Ayah's views. All he said was, 'We'll have to go away some day.'

'How long have we been here?' I asked.

'Two hundred years.'

'No, I mean us.'

'Well, you were born in India, so that's seven years for you.'

'Then can't I stay here?'

'Do you want to?'

'I want to go across the sea. But can we take Ayah with us?'

'I don't know, son. Let's walk along the beach.'

We lived in an old palace beside a lake. The palace looked like a ruin from the outside, but the rooms were cool and comfortable. We lived in one wing, and my father organized a small school in another wing. His pupils were the children of the raja and the raja's relatives. My father had started life in India as a tea planter, but he had been trained as a teacher and the idea of starting a school in a small state facing the Arabian Sea had appealed to him. The pay wasn't much, but we had a palace to live in, the latest 1938 model Hillman to drive about in and a number of servants. In those days, of course, everyone had servants (although the servants did not have any!). Ayah was our own; but the cook, the bearer, the gardener and the *bhisti* were all provided by the state.

Sometimes I sat in the schoolroom with the other children (who were all much bigger than me), sometimes I remained in the house with Ayah, sometimes I followed the gardener, Dukhi, about the spacious garden.

Dukhi means 'sad', and though I never could discover if the gardener had anything to feel sad about, the name certainly suited him. He had grown to resemble the drooping weeds that he was always digging up with a tiny spade. I seldom saw him standing up. He always sat on the ground with his knees well up to his chin, and attacked the weeds from this position. He could spend all day on his haunches, moving about the garden simply by shuffling his feet along the grass.

I tried to imitate his posture, sitting down on my heels and putting my knees into my armpits, but I could never hold the position for more than five minutes.

Time had no meaning in a large garden, and Dukhi never hurried. Life, for him, was not a matter of one year succeeding another, but of five seasons—winter, spring, hot weather, monsoon and autumn—arriving and departing. His seedbeds always had to be in readiness for the coming season, and he did not look any further than the next monsoon. It was impossible to tell his age. He may have been thirty-six or eighty-six. He was either very young for his years or very old for them.

Dukhi loved bright colours, especially reds and yellows. He liked strongly scented flowers, like jasmine and honeysuckle. He couldn't understand my father's preference for the more delicately perfumed petunias and sweetpeas. But I shared Dukhi's fondness for the common bright orange marigold, which is offered in temples and is used to make garlands and nosegays. When the garden was bare of all colour, the marigold would still be there, gay and flashy, challenging the sun.

Dukhi was very fond of making nosegays, and I liked to watch him at work. A sunflower formed the centrepiece. It was surrounded by roses, marigolds and oleander, fringed with green leaves and bound together with silver thread. The perfume was overpowering. The nosegays were presented to me or my father on special occasions, that is, on a birthday or to guests of my father's who were considered important.

One day I found Dukhi making a nosegay, and said, 'No one is coming today, Dukhi. It isn't even a birthday.'

'It is a birthday, Chota Sahib,' he said. 'Chota Sahib' was the title he had given me. It wasn't much of a title compared to Raja Sahib, Diwan Sahib or Burra Sahib, but it was nice to have a title at the age of seven.

'Oh,' I said. 'And is there a party, too?'

'No party.'

'What's the use of a birthday without a party? What's the use of a birthday without presents?'

'This person doesn't like presents—just flowers.'

'Who is it?' I asked, full of curiosity.

'If you want to find out, you can take these flowers to her. She lives right at the top of that far side of the palace. There are twenty-two steps to climb. Remember that, Chota Sahib, you take twenty-three steps and you will go over the edge and into the lake!'

I started climbing the stairs.

It was a spiral staircase of wrought iron, and it went round and round and up and up, and it made me quite dizzy and tired.

At the top I found myself on a small balcony, which looked out over the lake and another palace, at the crowded city and the distant harbour. I heard a voice, a rather high, musical voice, saying (in English), 'Are you a ghost?' I turned to see who had spoken but found the balcony empty. The voice had come from a dark room.

I turned to the stairway, ready to flee, but the voice said, 'Oh, don't go, there's nothing to be frightened of!'

And so I stood still, peering cautiously into the darkness of the room.

'First, tell me—are you a ghost?'

'I'm a boy,' I said.

'And I'm a girl. We can be friends. I can't come out there, so you had better come in. Come along, I'm not a ghost either—not yet, anyway!'

As there was nothing very frightening about the voice, I stepped into the room. It was dark inside, and coming in from the glare, it took me some time to make out the tiny, elderly lady seated on a cushioned gilt chair. She wore a red sari, lots of coloured bangles on her wrists and golden earrings. Her hair was streaked with white, but her skin was still quite smooth and unlined, and she had large and very beautiful eyes.

'You must be Master Bond!' she said. 'Do you know who I am?'

'You're a lady with a birthday,' I said, 'but that's all I know. Dukhi didn't tell me any more.'

'If you promise to keep it a secret, I'll tell you who I am. You see, everyone thinks I'm mad. Do you think so too?'

'I don't know.'

'Well, you must tell me if you think so,' she said with a chuckle. Her laugh was the sort of sound made by the gecko, a little wall lizard, coming from deep down in the throat. 'I have a feeling you are a truthful boy. Do you find it very difficult to tell the truth?'

'Sometimes.'

'Sometimes. Of course, there are times when I tell lies—lots of little lies—because they're such fun! But would you call me a liar? I wouldn't, if I were you, but would *you*?'

'Are you a liar?'

'I'm asking you! If I were to tell you that I was a queen—that I *am* a queen—would you believe me?'

I thought deeply about this, and then said, 'I'll try to believe you.'

'Oh, but you *must* believe me. I'm a real queen, I'm a rani! Look, I've got diamonds to prove it!' And she held out her hands and there was a ring on each finger, the stones glowing and glittering in the dim light. 'Diamonds, rubies, pearls and emeralds! Only a queen can have these!' She was most anxious that I should believe her.

'You must be a queen,' I said.

'Right!' she snapped. 'In that case, would you mind calling me "Your Highness"?'

'Your Highness,' I said.

She smiled. It was a slow, beautiful smile. Her whole face lit up.

'I could love you,' she said. 'But better still, I'll give you something to eat. Do you like chocolates?'

'Yes, Your Highness.'

'Well,' she said, taking a box from the table beside her, 'these have come all the way from England. Take two. Only two, mind, otherwise the box will finish before Thursday, and I don't want that to happen because I won't get any more till Saturday. That's when Captain MacWhirr's ship gets in, the *SS Lucy*, loaded with boxes and boxes of chocolates!'

'All for you?' I asked in considerable awe.

'Yes, of course. They have to last at least three months. I get them from England. I get only the best chocolates. I like them with pink crunchy fillings, don't you?'

'Oh, yes!' I exclaimed, full of envy.

'Never mind,' she said, 'I may give you one, now and then—if you're very nice to me! Here you are, help yourself...' She pushed the chocolate box towards me.

I took a silver-wrapped chocolate, and then just as I was thinking of taking a second, she quickly took the box away.

'No more!' she said. 'They have to last till Saturday.'

'But I took only *one*,' I said with some indignation.

'Did you?' She gave me a sharp look, decided I was telling the truth, and said graciously, 'Well, in that case you can have another.'

Watching the rani carefully, in case she snatched the box away again, I selected a second chocolate, this one with a green wrapper. I don't remember what kind of day it was outside, but I remember the bright green of the chocolate wrapper.

I thought it would be rude to eat the chocolates in front of a queen, so I put them in my pocket and said, 'I'd better go now. Ayah will be looking for me.'

'And when will you be coming to see me again?'

'I don't know,' I said.

'There's something I want you to do for me,' she said, placing one finger on my shoulder and giving me a conspiratorial look. 'Will you do it?'

'What is it, Your Highness?'

'What is it? Why do you ask? A real prince never asks where or why or whatever, he simply does what the princess asks of him. When I was a princess—before I became a queen, that is—I asked a prince to swim across the lake and fetch me a lily growing on the other bank.'

'And did he get it for you?'

'He drowned halfway across. Let that be a lesson to you. Never agree to do something without knowing what it is.'

'But I thought you said...'

'Never mind what I said. It's what I say that matters!'

'Oh, all right,' I said, fidgeting to be gone. 'What is it you want me to do?'

'Nothing.' Her tiny rosebud lips pouted and she stared sullenly at a picture on the wall. Now that my eyes had grown used to the dim light in the room, I noticed that the walls were hung with portraits of stout rajas and ranis, turbaned and bedecked in fine clothes. There were also portraits of Queen Victoria and King George V of England. And, in the centre of all this distinguished company, a large picture of Mickey Mouse.

'I'll do it if it isn't too dangerous,' I said.

'Then listen.' She took my hand and drew me towards her—what a tiny hand she had!—and whispered, 'I want a *red* rose from the palace garden. But be careful! Don't let Dukhi the gardener catch you. He'll know it's for me. He knows I love roses. And he hates me! I'll tell you why, one day. But if he catches you, he'll do something terrible.'

'To me?'

'No, to himself. That's much worse, isn't it? He'll tie himself into knots, or lie naked on a bed of thorns, or go on a long fast with nothing to eat but fruit, sweets and chicken! So you will be careful, won't you?'

'Oh, but he doesn't hate you,' I cried in protest, remembering the flowers he'd sent for her, and looking around I found that I'd been sitting on them. 'Look, he sent these flowers for your birthday!'

'Well, if he sent them for my birthday, you can take them back,' she snapped. 'But if he sent them for *me*...' and she suddenly softened and looked coy, 'then I might keep them. Thank you, my dear, it was a very sweet thought.' And she leaned forward as though to kiss me.

'It's late, I must go!' I said in alarm and, turning on my heels, ran out of the room and down the spiral staircase.

Father hadn't started lunch, or rather tiffin, as we called it then. He usually waited for me if I was late. I don't suppose he enjoyed eating alone.

For tiffin we usually had rice, mutton curry (koftas or meat balls, with plenty of gravy, was my favourite curry), fried dal and a hot lime or mango pickle. For supper, we had English food—a soup, roast pork and fried potatoes, a rich gravy made by my father and a custard or caramel pudding. My father enjoyed cooking, but it was only in the morning that he found time for it. Breakfast was his own creation. He cooked eggs in a variety of interesting ways, and favoured some Italian recipes which he had collected during a trip to Europe, long before I was born.

In deference to the feelings of our Hindu friends, we did not eat beef, but, apart from mutton and chicken, there was a plentiful supply of other meats—partridge, venison, lobster and even porcupine!

'And where have you been?' asked my father, helping himself to rice as soon as he saw me come in.

'To the top of the old palace,' I said.

'Did you meet anyone there?'

'Yes, I met a tiny lady who told me she was a rani. She gave me chocolates.'

'As a rule, she doesn't like visitors.'

'Oh, she didn't mind me. But is she really a queen?'

'Well, she's the daughter of a maharaja. That makes her a princess. She never married. There's a story that she fell in love with a commoner, one of the palace servants, and wanted to marry him, but of course they wouldn't allow that. She became very melancholic, and started living all by herself in the old palace. They give her everything she needs, but she doesn't go out or have visitors. Everyone says she's mad.'

'How do they know?' I asked.

'Because she's different from other people, I suppose.'

'Is that being mad?'

'No. Not really, I suppose madness is not seeing things as others see them.'

'Is that very bad?'

'No,' said Father, who for once was finding it very difficult to explain something to me. 'But people who are like that—people whose minds are so different that they don't think, step by step, as we do, whose thoughts jump all over the place—such people are very difficult to live with...'

'Step by step,' I repeated. 'Step by step...'

'You aren't eating,' said my father. 'Hurry up, and you can come with me to school today.'

I always looked forward to attending my father's classes. He did not take me to the schoolroom very often, because he wanted school to be a treat, to begin with, and then later the routine wouldn't be so unwelcome.

Sitting there with older children, understanding only half of what they were learning, I felt important and part grown-up. And of course I did learn to read and write, although I first learnt to read upside-down, by means of standing in front of the others' desks and peering across at their books. Later, when I went to school, I had some difficulty in learning to read the right way up; and even today I sometimes read upside-down, for the sake of variety. I don't mean that I read standing on my head, simply that I held the book upside-down.

I had at my command a number of rhymes and jingles, the most interesting of these being 'Solomon Grundy'.

Solomon Grundy,
Born on a Monday,
Christened on Tuesday,
Married on Wednesday,
Took ill on Thursday,
Worse on Friday,
Died on Saturday,
Buried on Sunday:
This is the end of
Solomon Grundy.

Was that all that life amounted to, in the end? And were we all Solomon Grundys? These were questions that bothered me at the time. Another puzzling rhyme was the one that went:

Hark, hark,
The dogs do bark,
The beggars are coming to town;
Some in rags,
Some in bags,
And some in velvet gowns.

This rhyme puzzled me for a long time. There were beggars aplenty in the bazaar, and sometimes they came to the house, and some of them did wear rags and bags (and some nothing at all) and the dogs did bark at them, but the beggar in the velvet gown never came our way.

'Who's this beggar in a velvet gown?' I asked my father.

'Not a beggar at all,' he said.

'Then why call him one?'

And I went to Ayah and asked her the same question, 'Who is the beggar in the velvet gown?'

'Jesus Christ,' said Ayah.

Ayah was a fervent Christian and made me say my prayers at night, even when I was very sleepy. She had, I think, Arab and Negro blood in addition to the blood of the Koli fishing community to which her mother had belonged. Her father, a sailor on an Arab dhow, had been a convert to Christianity. Ayah was a large, buxom woman, with heavy hands and feet and a slow, swaying gait that had all the grace and majesty of a royal elephant. Elephants for all their size are nimble creatures, and Ayah, too, was nimble, sensitive and gentle with her big hands. Her face was always sweet and childlike.

Although a Christian, she clung to many of the beliefs of her parents and loved to tell me stories about mischievous spirits and evil spirits, humans who changed into animals, and snakes who had been princes in their former lives.

There was the story of the snake who married a princess. At first the princess did not wish to marry the snake, whom she had met in a forest, but the snake insisted saying, 'I'll kill you if you won't marry me,' and of course that settled the question. The snake led his bride away and took her to a great treasure. 'I was a prince in my former life,' he explained. 'This treasure is yours.' And then the snake very gallantly disappeared.

'Snakes,' declared Ayah, 'were very lucky omens if seen early in the morning.'

'But, what if the snake bites the lucky person?' I asked.

'He will be lucky all the same,' said Ayah with a logic that was all her own.

Snakes! There were a number of them living in the big garden, and my father had advised me to avoid the long grass. But I had seen snakes crossing the road (a lucky omen, according to Ayah) and they were never aggressive.

'A snake won't attack you,' said Father, 'provided you leave it alone. Of course, if you step on one it will probably bite.'

'Are all snakes poisonous?'

'Yes, but only a few are poisonous enough to kill a man. Others use their poison on rats and frogs. A good thing, too, otherwise during the rains the house would be taken over by the frogs.'

One afternoon, while Father was at school, Ayah found a snake in the bathtub. It wasn't early morning and so the snake couldn't have been a lucky one. Ayah was frightened and ran into the garden calling for help. Dukhi came running. Ayah ordered me to stay outside while they went after the snake.

And it was while I was alone in the garden—an unusual circumstance, since Dukhi was nearly always there—that I remembered the rani's request. On an impulse, I went to the nearest rose bush and plucked the largest rose, pricking my thumb in the process.

And then, without waiting to see what had happened to the snake (it finally escaped), I started up the steps to the top of the old palace.

When I got to the top, I knocked on the door of the rani's room. Getting no reply, I walked along the balcony until I reached another doorway. There were wooden panels around the door, with elephants, camels and turbaned warriors carved into it. As the door was open, I walked boldly into the room then stood still in astonishment. The room was filled with a strange light.

There were windows going right round the room, and each small windowpane was made of a different coloured glass. The sun that came through one window flung red and green and purple colours on the figure of the little rani who stood there with her face pressed to the glass.

She spoke to me without turning from the window. 'This is

my favourite room. I have all the colours here. I can see a different world through each pane of glass. Come, join me!' And she beckoned to me, her small hand fluttering like a delicate butterfly.

I went up to the rani. She was only a little taller than me, and we were able to share the same windowpane.

'See, it's a red world!' she said.

The garden below, the palace and the lake were all tinted red. I watched the rani's world for a little while and then touched her on the arm and said, 'I have brought you a rose!'

She started away from me, and her eyes looked frightened. She would not look at the rose.

'Oh, why did you bring it?' she cried, wringing her hands. 'He'll be arrested now!'

'Who'll be arrested?'

'The prince, of course!'

'But *I* took it,' I said. 'No one saw me. Ayah and Dukhi were inside the house, catching a snake.'

'Did they catch it?' she asked, forgetting about the rose.

'I don't know. I didn't wait to see!'

'They should follow the snake, instead of catching it. It may lead them to a treasure. All snakes have treasures to guard.'

This seemed to confirm what Ayah had been telling me, and I resolved that I would follow the next snake that I met.

'Don't you like the rose, then?' I asked.

'Did you steal it?'

'Yes.'

'Good. Flowers should always be stolen. They're more fragrant then.'

Because of a man called Hitler, war had been declared in Europe and Britain was fighting Germany.

In my comic papers, the Germans were usually shown as blundering idiots; so I didn't see how Britain could possibly lose the War, nor why it should concern India, nor why it should be necessary for my father to join up. But I remember him showing me a newspaper headline that said:

BOMBS FALL ON BUCKINGHAM PALACE—
KING AND QUEEN SAFE

I expect that had something to do with it.

He went to Delhi for an interview with the RAF and I was left in Ayah's charge.

It was a week I remember well, because it was the first time I had been left on my own. That first night I was afraid—afraid of the dark, afraid of the emptiness of the house, afraid of the howling of the jackals outside. The loud ticking of the clock was the only reassuring sound: clocks really made themselves heard in those days! I tried concentrating on the ticking, shutting out other sounds and the menace of the dark, but it wouldn't work. I thought I heard a faint hissing near the bed, and sat up, bathed in perspiration, certain that a snake was in the room. I shouted for Ayah and she came running, switching on all the lights.

'A snake!' I cried. 'There's a snake in the room!'

'Where, baba?'

'I don't know where, but I *heard* it.'

Ayah looked under the bed, and behind the chairs and tables, but there was no snake to be found. She persuaded me that I must have heard the breeze whispering in the mosquito curtains.

But I didn't want to be left alone.

'I'm coming to you,' I said and followed her into her small room near the kitchen.

Ayah slept on a low string cot. The mattress was thin, the blanket worn and patched up; but Ayah's warm and solid body made up for the discomfort of the bed. I snuggled up to her and was soon asleep.

I had almost forgotten the rani in the old palace and was about to pay her a visit when, to my surprise, I found her in the garden. I had risen early that morning, and had gone running barefoot over the dew-drenched grass. No one was about, but I startled a flock of parrots and the birds rose screeching from a banyan tree and wheeled away to some other corner of the palace grounds. I was just in time to see a mongoose scurrying across the grass with an egg in its mouth. The mongoose must have been raiding the poultry farm at the palace.

I was trying to locate the mongoose's hideout, and was on all fours in a jungle of tall cosmos plants when I heard the rustle of clothes, and turned to find the rani staring at me.

She didn't ask me what I was doing there, but simply said: 'I don't think he could have gone in there.'

'But I saw him go this way,' I said.

'Nonsense! He doesn't live in this part of the garden. He lives in the roots of the banyan tree.'

'But that's where the snake lives,' I said.

'You mean the snake who was a prince. Well, that's whom I'm looking for!'

'A snake who was a prince!' I gaped at the rani.

She made a gesture of impatience with her butterfly hands, and said, 'Tut, you're only a child, you can't understand. The prince lives in the roots of the banyan tree, but he comes out early every morning. Have you seen him?'

'No. But I saw a mongoose.'

The rani became frightened. 'Oh dear, is there a mongoose in the garden? He might kill the prince!'

'How can a mongoose kill a prince?' I asked.

'You don't understand, Master Bond. Princes, when they die, are born again as snakes.'

'*All* princes?'

'No, only those who die before they can marry.'

'Did your prince die before he could marry you?'

'Yes. And he returned to this garden in the form of a beautiful snake.'

'Well,' I said, 'I hope it wasn't the snake the water carrier killed last week.'

'He killed a snake!' The rani looked horrified. She was quivering all over. 'It might have been the prince!'

'It was a brown snake,' I said.

'Oh, then it wasn't him.' She looked very relieved. 'Brown snakes are only ministers and people like that. It has to be a green snake to be a prince.'

'I haven't seen any green snakes here.'

'There's one living in the roots of the banyan tree. You won't kill it, will you?'

'Not if it's really a prince.'

'And you won't let others kill it?'

'I'll tell Ayah.'

'Good. You're on my side. But be careful of the gardener. Keep him away from the banyan tree. He's always killing snakes. I don't trust him at all.'

She came nearer and, leaning forward a little, looked into my eyes.

'Blue eyes—I trust them. But don't trust green eyes. And yellow eyes are evil.'

'I've never seen yellow eyes.'

'That's because you're pure,' she said and turned away and hurried across the lawn as though she had just remembered a very urgent appointment.

The sun was up, slanting through the branches of the banyan tree, and Ayah's voice could be heard calling me for breakfast.

'Dukhi,' I said, when I found him in the garden later that day, 'don't kill the snake in the banyan tree.'

'A snake in the banyan tree!' he exclaimed, seizing his hose.

'No, no!' I said. 'I haven't seen it. But the rani says there's one. She says it was a prince in its former life, and that we shouldn't kill it.'

'Oh,' said Dukhi, smiling to himself. 'The rani says so. All right, you tell her we won't kill it.'

'Is it true that she was in love with a prince but that he died before she could marry him?'

'Something like that,' said Dukhi. 'It was a long time ago—before I came here.'

'My father says it wasn't a prince, but a commoner. Are you a commoner, Dukhi?'

'A commoner? What's that, Chota Sahib?'

'I'm not sure. Someone very poor, I suppose.'

'Then I must be a commoner,' said Dukhi.

'Were you in love with the rani?' I asked.

Dukhi was so startled that he dropped his hose and lost his balance; the first time I'd seen him lose his poise while squatting on his haunches.

'Don't say such things, Chota Sahib!'

'Why not?'

'You'll get me into trouble.'

'Then it must be true.'

Dukhi threw up his hands in mock despair and started collecting his implements.

'It's true, it's true!' I cried, dancing round him, and then I ran indoors to Ayah and said, 'Ayah, Dukhi was in love with the rani!'

Ayah gave a shriek of laughter, then looked very serious and put her finger against my lips.

'Don't say such things,' she said. 'Dukhi is of a very low caste. People won't like it if they hear what you say. And besides, the rani told you her prince died and turned into a snake. Well, Dukhi hasn't become a snake as yet, has he?'

True, Dukhi didn't look as though he could be anything but a gardener; but I wasn't satisfied with his denials or with Ayah's attempts to still my tongue. Hadn't Dukhi sent the rani a nosegay?

When my father came home, he looked quite pleased with himself.

'What have you brought for me?' was the first question I asked.

He had brought me some new books, a dartboard and a train set; and in my excitement over examining these gifts, I forgot to ask about the result of his trip.

It was during tiffin that he told me what had happened—and what was going to happen.

'We'll be going away soon,' he said. 'I've joined the Royal Air Force. I'll have to work in Delhi.'

'Oh! Will you be in the War, Dad? Will you fly a plane?'

'No, I'm too old to be flying planes. I'll be forty years old in July. The RAF will be giving me what they call intelligence work—decoding secret messages and things like that and I don't suppose I'll be able to tell you much about it.'

This didn't sound as exciting as flying planes, but it sounded important and rather mysterious.

'Well, I hope it's interesting,' I said. 'Is Delhi a good place to live in?'

'I'm not sure. It will be very hot by the middle of April. And you won't be able to stay with me, Ruskin—not at first, anyway, not until I can get married quarters and then, only if your mother returns... Meanwhile, you'll stay with your grandmother in Dehra.' He must have seen the disappointment in my face, because he quickly added: 'Of course, I'll come to see you often. Dehra isn't far from Delhi—only a night's train journey.'

But I was dismayed. It wasn't that I didn't want to stay with my grandmother, but I had grown so used to sharing my father's life and even watching him at work, that the thought of being separated from him was unbearable.

'Not as bad as going to boarding school,' he said. 'And that's the only alternative.'

'Not boarding school,' I said quickly, 'I'll run away from boarding school.'

'Well, you won't want to run away from your grandmother. She's very fond of you. And if you come with me to Delhi, you'll be alone all day in a stuffy little hut while I'm away at work. Sometimes I may have to go on tour—then what happens?'

'I don't mind being on my own.' And this was true. I had already grown accustomed to having my own room and my own trunk and my own bookshelf and I felt as though I was about to lose these things.

'Will Ayah come too?' I asked.

My father looked thoughtful. 'Would you like that?'

'Ayah must come,' I said firmly. 'Otherwise I'll run away.'

'I'll have to ask her,' said my father.

Ayah, it turned out, was quite ready to come with us. In fact, she was indignant that Father should have considered leaving her behind. She had brought me up since my mother went away, and she wasn't going to hand over charge to any upstart aunt or governess. She was pleased and excited at the prospect of the move, and this helped to raise my spirits.

'What is Dehra like?' I asked my father.

'It's a green place,' he said. 'It lies in a valley in the foothills of the Himalayas and it's surrounded by forests. There are lots of trees in Dehra.'

'Does Grandmother's house have trees?'

'Yes. There's a big jackfruit tree in the garden. Your grandmother planted it when I was a boy. And there's an old banyan tree, which is good to climb. And there are fruit trees, litchis, mangoes, papayas.'

'Are there any books?'

'Grandmother's books won't interest you. But I'll be bringing you books from Delhi whenever I come to see you.'

I was beginning to look forward to the move. Changing houses had always been fun. Changing towns ought to be fun, too.

A few days before we left, I went to say goodbye to the rani.

'I'm going away,' I said.

'How lovely!' said the rani. 'I wish I could go away!'

'Why don't you?'

'They won't let me. They're afraid to let me out of the palace.'

'What are they afraid of, Your Highness?'

'That I might run away. Run away, far, far away, to the land where the leopards are learning to pray.'

Gosh, I thought, she's really quite crazy… But then she was silent, and started smoking a small hookah.

She drew on the hookah, looked at me, and asked, 'Where is your mother?'

'I haven't one.'

'Everyone has a mother. Did yours die?'

'No. She went away.'

She drew on her hookah again and then said, very sweetly, 'Don't go away…'

'I must,' I said. 'It's because of the War.'

'What war? Is there a war on? You see, no one tells me anything.'

'It's between us and Hitler,' I said.

'And who is Hitler?'

'He's a German.'

'I knew a German once, Dr Schreinherr, he had beautiful hands.'

'Was he an artist?'

'He was a dentist.'

The rani got up from her couch and accompanied me out on to the balcony. When we looked down at the garden, we could see Dukhi weeding a flower bed. Both of us gazed down at him in silence, and I wondered what the rani would say if I asked her if she had ever been in love with the palace gardener. Ayah had told me it would be an insulting question, so I held my peace. But as I walked slowly down the spiral staircase, the rani's voice came after me.

'Thank him,' she said. 'Thank him for the beautiful rose.'

THE OLD GRAMOPHONE

It was a large square mahogany box, well polished, and there was a handle you had to wind, and lids that opened top and front. You changed the steel needle every time you changed the record.

The records were kept flat in a cardboard box to prevent them from warping. If you didn't pack them flat, the heat and humidity turned them into strange shapes which would have made them eligible for an exhibition of modern sculpture.

The winding, the changing of records and needles, the selection of a record were boyhood tasks that I thoroughly enjoyed. I was very methodical in these matters. I hated records being scratched, or the turntable slowing down in the middle of a record, bringing the music of the song to a slow and mournful stop: this happened if the gramophone wasn't fully wound. I was especially careful with my favourites, such as Nelson Eddy singing 'The Mounties' and 'The Hills of Home', various numbers sung by the Ink Spots, and medley of marches.

All this musical activity (requiring much physical exertion on the part of the listener!) took place in a little-known port called Jamnagar, on the west coast of our country, where my father taught English to the young princes and princesses of the state. The gramophone had been installed to amuse me and my mother, but my mother couldn't be bothered with all the effort that went into playing it.

I loved every aspect of the gramophone, even the cleaning of the records with a special cloth. One of my first feats of writing was to catalogue all the records in our collection—only about fifty to begin with—and this cataloguing I did with great care and devotion. My father liked 'grand opera'—Caruso, Gigli and Galli-Curci—but I preferred the lighter ballads of Nelson Eddy, Deanna Durbin, Gracie Fields, Richard Tauber, and 'The Street Singer' (Arthur Tracy). It may seem incongruous, to have been living within sound of the Arabian Sea and listening to Nelson sing most beautifully of the mighty Missouri river, but it was perfectly natural to me. I grew up with that music, and I love it still.

I was a lonely boy, without friends of my own age, so that the gramophone and the record collection meant a lot to me. My catalogue went into new and longer editions, taking in the names of composers, lyricists and accompanists.

When we left Jamnagar, the gramophone accompanied us on the long train journey (three days and three nights, with several changes) to Dehradun. Here, in the spacious grounds of my grandparents' home at the foothills of the Himalayas, songs like 'The Hills of Home' and 'Shenandoah' did not seem out of place.

Grandfather had a smaller gramophone and a record collection of his own. His tastes were more 'modern' than mine. Dance music was his passion, and there were any number of foxtrots, tangos and beguines played by the leading dance bands of the 1940s. Granny preferred waltzes and taught me to waltz. I would waltz with her on the broad veranda, to the strains of 'The Blue Danube' and 'The Skater's Waltz', while a soft breeze rustled in the banana fronds. I became quite good at the waltz, but then I saw Gene Kelly tap-dancing in a brash, colourful MGM musical, and—base treachery!—forsook the waltz and began tap-dancing all over the house, much to Granny's dismay.

All this is pure nostalgia, of course, but why be ashamed of it? Nostalgia is simply an attempt to try and preserve that which was good in the past… The past has served us: why not serve the past in this way?

When I was sent to boarding school and was away from home for nine long months, I really missed the gramophone. How I looked forward to coming home for the winter holidays! There were, of course, some new records waiting for me. And Grandfather had taken to the Brazilian rumba, which was all the rage just then. Yes, Grandfather did the rumba with great aplomb.

I believe he moved on to the samba and then the calypso, but by then I'd left India and was away for five years. A great deal had changed in my absence. My grandparents had moved on, and my mother had sold the old gramophone and replaced it with a large radiogram. But this wasn't so much fun: I wanted something I could wind!

I keep hoping our old gramophone will turn up somewhere—maybe in an antique shop or in someone's attic or storeroom, or at a sale. Then I shall buy it back, whatever the cost, and install it in my study and have the time of my life winding it up and playing the old records. I now have tapes of some of them, but that won't stop me listening to the gramophone. I have even kept a box of needles in readiness for the great day.

THE PHOTOGRAPH

I was ten years old. My grandmother sat on the string bed under the mango tree. It was late summer and there were sunflowers in the garden and a warm wind in the trees. My grandmother was knitting a woollen scarf for the winter months. She was very old, dressed in a plain white sari. Her eyes were not very strong now but her fingers moved quickly with the needles and the needles kept clicking all afternoon. Grandmother had white hair but there were very few wrinkles on her skin.

I had come home after playing cricket in the maidan. I had taken my meal and now I was rummaging through a box of old books and family heirlooms that had just that day been brought out of the attic by my mother. Nothing in the box interested me very much except for a book with colourful pictures of birds and butterflies. I was going through the book, looking at the pictures, when I found a small photograph between the pages. It was a faded picture, a little yellow and foggy. It was the picture of a girl standing against a wall and behind the wall there was nothing but sky. But from the other side a pair of hands reached up, as though someone was going to climb the wall. There were flowers growing near the girl but I couldn't tell what they were. There was a creeper too but it was just a creeper.

I ran out into the garden. 'Granny!' I shouted. 'Look at this picture! I found it in the box of old things. Whose picture is it?'

I jumped on the bed beside my grandmother and she

walloped me on the bottom and said, 'Now I've lost count of my stitches and the next time you do that I'll make you finish the scarf yourself.'

Granny was always threatening to teach me how to knit which I thought was a disgraceful thing for a boy to do. It was a good deterrent for keeping me out of mischief. Once I had torn the drawing-room curtains and Granny had put a needle and thread in my hand and made me stitch the curtain together, even though I made long, two-inch stitches, which had to be taken out by my mother and done again.

She took the photograph from my hand and we both stared at it for quite a long time. The girl had long, loose hair and she wore a long dress that nearly covered her ankles, and sleeves that reached her wrists, and there were a lot of bangles on her hands. But despite all this drapery, the girl appeared to be full of freedom and movement. She stood with her legs apart and her hands on her hips and had a wide, almost devilish smile on her face.

'Whose picture is it?' I asked.

'A little girl's, of course,' said Grandmother. 'Can't you tell?'

'Yes, but did you know the girl?'

'Yes, I knew her,' said Granny, 'but she was a very wicked girl and I shouldn't tell you about her. But I'll tell you about the photograph. It was taken in your grandfather's house about sixty years ago. And that's the garden wall and over the wall there was a road going to town.'

'Whose hands are they,' I asked, 'coming up from the other side?'

Grandmother squinted and looked closely at the picture, and shook her head. 'It's the first time I've noticed,' she said. 'They must have been the sweeper boy's. Or maybe they were your grandfather's.'

'They don't look like Grandfather's hands,' I said. 'His hands are all bony.'

'Yes, but this was sixty years ago.'

'Didn't he climb up the wall after the photo?'

'No, nobody climbed up. At least, I don't remember.'

'And you remember well, Granny.'

'Yes, I remember…I remember what is not in the photograph. It was a spring day and there was a cool breeze blowing, nothing like this. Those flowers at the girl's feet, they were marigolds, and the bougainvillea creeper, it was a mass of purple. You cannot see these colours in the photo and even if you could, as nowadays, you wouldn't be able to smell the flowers or feel the breeze.'

'And what about the girl?' I said. 'Tell me about the girl.'

'Well, she was a wicked girl,' said Granny. 'You don't know the trouble they had getting her into those fine clothes she's wearing.'

'I think they are terrible clothes,' I said.

'So did she. Most of the time, she hardly wore a thing. She used to go swimming in a muddy pool with a lot of ruffianly boys, and ride on the backs of buffaloes. No boy ever teased her, though, because she could kick and scratch and pull his hair out!'

'She looks like it too,' I said. 'You can tell by the way she's smiling. At any moment something's going to happen.'

'Something did happen,' said Granny. 'Her mother wouldn't let her take off the clothes afterwards, so she went swimming in them and lay for half an hour in the mud.'

I laughed heartily and Grandmother laughed too.

'Who was the girl?' I said. 'You must tell me who she was.'

'No, that wouldn't do,' said Grandmother, but I pretended I didn't know. I knew, because Grandmother still smiled in the same way, even though she didn't have as many teeth.

'Come on, Granny,' I said, 'tell me, tell me.'

But Grandmother shook her head and carried on with the knitting. And I held the photograph in my hand looking from it to my grandmother and back again, trying to find points in common between the old lady and the little pigtailed girl. A lemon-coloured butterfly settled on the end of Grandmother's knitting needle and stayed there while the needles clicked away. I made a grab at the butterfly and it flew off in a dipping flight and settled on a sunflower.

'I wonder whose hands they were,' whispered Grandmother to herself, with her head bowed, and her needles clicking away in the soft, warm silence of that summer afternoon.

THE BAR THAT TIME FORGOT

'Cockroaches!' exclaimed Her Highness the Maharani. 'Cockroaches everywhere! Can't put down my glass without finding a cockroach beneath it!'

'Cockroaches have a special liking for this room,' observed Colonel Wilkie, from his corner by the disused fireplace. 'For one thing, our Melaram there'—and he indicated the bartender with a tilt of his double chin—'never washes the glasses properly. And there are sandwich remains all over the place. Last week's sandwiches, I might add. From that party of yours, Krishan.'

Krishan, former Test cricketer, now forty and with a forty-three-inch waist, turned to the colonel. 'You should see the kitchen. A pigsty. The cook is seldom sober.'

'*We* are seldom sober,' said Suresh Mathur, income-tax lawyer, from his favourite bar stool.

'Speak for yourself,' snapped H.H. 'Simon, fetch me another whisky.'

Simon Lee, secretary-companion to Her Highness, rose dutifully from his chair and took her glass over to the bar counter.

'Indian whisky or Scotch, sir?' asked the bartender in a loud voice, knowing the Maharani was too mean to buy Scotch.

'Whisky will do,' said Simon. 'And a beer for me.' Just then he felt like spiking the Maharani's whisky with something really lethal, and be free of her for the rest of his days. Years of loyalty and companionship had given way to abject slavery, and there was nothing he could do about it. Nearing seventy, unqualified and unworldly, he could hardly set about creating any sort of career for himself.

'And what are *you* having?' he asked Suresh Mathur, who had just put away his first drink.

'I am never vague, I ask for Haig!' Suresh replied, chuckling at his clever rhyme. None of the others thought it amusing, but this was usual. 'When they stop giving me credit, I'll try the local stuff.'

'Good on you!' called Colonel Wilkie from his corner. 'But there's nothing to beat Solan No. 1. Don't trust these single malts—they always give one gout!'

'I've never seen you move from that chair,' said Krishan. 'No wonder you suffer from gout.'

'Played cricket once, like you,' said the Colonel. 'Made a few runs. But they always made me twelfth man. Got fed up of carrying out the drinks, or fielding when the star batsman felt indisposed. Gave up cricket. Indoor games are better. Why don't we have a dartboard in here? In England, every respectable pub has a dartboard.'

I'd been listening to the conversation from a small table behind a potted palm. I was sixteen, just out of school, and I wasn't supposed to be in the bar, even if I wasn't drinking. The large potted palm separated the bar-room from the outer lounge; it was neutral territory.

'I have a dartboard!' I piped up, and every head turned towards me. Most of them had been unaware of my presence. They knew, of course, that I was the son of the lady who managed the hotel.

Suresh Mathur, the most literary-inclined of the lot, said: 'Young Copperfield has a dartboard!'

'I'll go and fetch it,' I said, only too ready to justify my presence in the bar.

I dashed down the corridor to my room and collided with my mother who was doing her nightly round of the hotel.

'What are you doing here? You mustn't hang around the bar,' she said sharply. 'You have a radio in your room, apart from all your books.'

The radio had been given to me the previous year by a guest who was now wanted by the police (on suspicion of being a serial killer), but I did not feel in any way guilty about possessing it; the guest had been very friendly and generous.

'Darts,' I told my mother. 'They want to play darts. That's what a pub is for, isn't it?' And I charged into my room, picked up my old dartboard and set of darts, and returned breathless to the bar-room.

My arrival was greeted by cheers, and Krishan helped me find a place for the dartboard, just below a framed picture of winged cherubs sporting about on some unlikely clouds.

'Whoever gets the highest score gets a free drink,' announced Krishan.

'Who pays for it?' asked Suresh Mathur.

'We all do—income-tax lawyers included.'

'He never saved anyone a rupee of tax,' declared the Maharani. 'But come on, let's have a game.'

'Would you like to start the proceedings, H.H.?'

'No, I'll wait till everyone's finished. You can start with Colonel Wilkie.'

'Age before beauty,' said Krishan. 'Come on, Colonel, we know you have a steady hand.'

Colonel Wilkie's hand was far from steady. His hands were always trembling. But he struggled out of his chair and took up his position at a point indicated by Krishan. Only one of his darts struck the board, earning him fifteen points. The others were near misses. Two darts bounced off the picture on the wall.

'The old fool's aiming at those naked cherubs,' crowed H.H. 'Go on, Simon, see if you can win a free drink for me.'

Simon did his best, but scored a meagre thirty points.

'Idiot!' cried H.H. 'And you always said you were a good darts player.'

'Out of practice,' Simon mumbled.

Meanwhile, someone had opened up the old radiogram and placed a record on the turntable. The cheeky voice of Maurice Chevalier filled the room:

All I want is just one girl,
But I have to have one girl
All I want is one
For a start!

The evening was livening up. Suresh Mathur scored a few points, but it was Krishan who hit the bullseye and claimed a drink on the house.

'Not until I've had my turn,' shouted H.H., and made a grab for the darts.

She flung them at the board at random, missing wildly—so much so that one dart lodged itself in Colonel Wilkie's old felt hat which was hanging from a peg, while another streaked across the room and narrowly missed the Roman nose of Reggie Bhowmik, ex-actor, who had just entered the room accompanied by his demure little wife.

Between ex-actor Reggie and former cricketer Krishan there was no love lost. Both middle aged and no longer in demand, they were rivals in failure. One spoke of the prejudice and incompetence of the cricket selectors, the other of jealousy in the film industry and his subsequent neglect. Both lived in the past—Krishan recalling the one outstanding innings he had played for the country (before being dropped after a series of failures), Reggie living on memories of his one great romantic role before a sagging waistline and alcohol-coarsened features had led to a rapid decline in his popularity. Somehow they had drifted into the backwater that was Dehra in 1950.

There are some places, no matter how dull or lacking in opportunity, which nevertheless take a grip on the individual, especially the more easy-going types, and hold him in thrall, rendering him unfit for life in a larger, more competitive milieu. Dehra was one such place.

The bar at Green's Hotel was their refuge and their strength. Here they could reminisce, hark back to glory days, even speak optimistically of the future. Colonel Wilkie, Suresh Mathur, Krishan Kapoor, Reggie Bhowmik, H.H.—the Maharani—and Simon Lee, were all dropouts, failures in their own way. Had they been busy and successful, they would not have found their way to Green's every evening.

Reggie Bhowmik liked making dramatic entrances, but the Maharani was just as fond of being the centre of attention, and wasn't about to give up centre stage to a fading actor.

'A double whisky for Krishan!' she declared. 'He's the only one here who still has a steady hand.'

'You haven't felt *my* hand,' said Reggie, bearing down on her. 'You missed my nose by a whisker.'

'You'd look better with a scar running down your face,' said H.H. 'Then you might get a role as Frankenstein or the phantom of the opera.'

This touched a raw nerve, as Reggie had been having some difficulty in getting a decent role in recent months. But he snapped back: 'I'll play the phantom on condition that you're cast as the fat soprano—then I shall take great pleasure in strangling you.'

'Let's change the subject,' said his wife Ruby, always ready to pour oil on troubled waters. She moved over to Colonel Wilkie's table and asked: 'How have you been, Colonel?'

'Like an old bus just about moving, and badly in need of spare parts.'

'Well, have a beer with us—and some French fries if we can get any.'

'Cook's on strike,' said Krishan. 'Only liquid diet today.' I saw my opportunity, and piped up again from behind the potted palm. 'I can boil some eggs for you if you like!' There was a stunned silence, broken by Suresh Mathur who said, sounding a little incredulous, 'Young Master Copperfield can boil an egg!'

Everyone clapped, and Krishan said, 'Copperfield has certainly saved the day for us. First he produces a dartboard, and now he's about to save us from starvation. Go to it, Copperfield!'

Off I went, then, not to boil eggs—there weren't any in the kitchen—but to find Sitaram, the room-boy, who was the only person of my age in the hotel. I found him in my room, listening to 'Binaca Geetmala', the popular musical request programme, on my radio.

'We need some eggs,' I told him. 'Boiled.'

'Egg-man comes tomorrow,' he said. 'Cook finished the rest. Made himself an omelette, got drunk, and took off!'

'Well, let's go down to the bazaar and buy some eggs. I've got enough money on me.'

So off we went, and near the clock tower found a street vendor selling boiled eggs. We bought a dozen and hurried back to the bar-room, where Krishan and Reggie were having a heated argument on the relative merits of cricket and football. Reggie didn't think much of cricket, and Krishan didn't think much of football.

'And what's *your* favourite game?' asked Ruby of Suresh Mathur.

'Snakes and ladders,' he said, chuckling, and returned to his drink.

'Boiled eggs!' I announced. 'On the house!'

Sitaram produced saucers, and distributed the eggs among the guests—two each, exactly.

'Do I have to peel my own egg?' asked the Maharani querulously, staring down at the two eggs rolling about on her plate. 'Peel them for me, Simon!'

Simon dutifully cracked one of the eggs and began peeling it for her. 'Not that way, you fool. You're leaving all the skin on it.' And seizing the half-peeled egg from her companion, she flung it across the room, narrowly missing the bartender.

'Good throw!' exclaimed Krishan. 'You'd be great fielding on the boundary.'

'Better at baseball,' said Reggie.

'Snakes and ladders,' said Suresh again, now quite drunk.

Colonel Wilkie, equally drunk, gave a loud belch.

The Maharani got up to leave. 'Well, I'm not going to sit here to be insulted by everyone. Come on, Simon, drive me home!' And she marched out of the room with an attempt at majesty, but tripped over the hotel cat, an ugly, striped creature who had sensed that there was food around and had come looking for it. The cat caterwauled, H.H. screamed and cursed, Reggie cheered, and Suresh Mather pronounced, 'When two cats are fighting they make a hideous sound.'

Not to be outdone in nastiness, the Maharani went up to Suresh, looked him up and down, and said, 'It's easy to tell you're a single man.'

'I'm not homosexual,' said Suresh defensively. (The word 'gay' had yet to be used in any sense other than 'happy' in those days.)

'No,' the Maharani smiled wickedly. 'You're single because you are so damn ugly!'

And on that triumphant note she left the room, followed by the obedient Simon.

'Pay no attention to her, Suresh,' said Krishan generously. 'You're better-looking than that old lapdog who follows her around.'

'I understand she's leaving him her fortunes,' said Reggie. 'I could do with some of it myself. Perhaps I could interest her in producing a film.'

'She's tight-fisted,' said Krishan. 'If you look closely at Simon you'll notice he's wearing the late Maharaja's smoking jacket and deerstalker cap. The old Maharaja loved dressing up like Sherlock Holmes.'

Colonel Wilkie came out of his reverie. 'When I was in Jamnagar—' he began.

'We've heard that a hundred times,' said Krishan.

'*I* haven't,' said Ruby.

'When I was in Jamnagar,' continued Colonel Wilkie, 'I saw Duleep Singh ji make a hundred. That was against Lord Tennyson's team.'

'Yesterday you said Ranjit Singh ji,' remarked Krishan.

'I'm not that old,' said Colonel Wilkie, struggling to his feet. 'But old enough to want to go to bed. I'll toddle off now.' Locating his walking-stick, he found his way to the door, wishing everyone goodnight as he passed them. They heard the tap of his walking stick as he walked away down the corridor.

'Shouldn't someone go with him?' asked Ruby. 'It's very late and he isn't too steady on his feet.'

'Oh, he'll find his way home,' said Suresh nonchalantly. 'Lives just around the corner, in rented rooms near the Club.'

'Why doesn't he join the Club?'

'Can't afford it. Neither can I.'

'Neither can I,' said Krishan.

'Neither can we,' added Ruby, sadly. 'And anyway, it's more homely here. Even when the Maharani is around.'

'*She* can afford the Club,' said Suresh. 'But they won't let her in. Created a disturbance once too often. Insulted the secretary and emptied a dish of chicken biryani on his head.'

'Not done,' said Krishan. 'Not cricket.'

'I don't believe it,' said Reggie. 'Can't be true.'

'Calling me a liar?' asked Suresh, bristling.

Ruby poured oil on troubled waters again. 'Interesting if true,' she said. 'And if not true, still interesting.'

'Mark Twain.'

My mother came along the corridor just as Krishan had shown off his knowledge of literature, and found me behind the palms listening to all this fascinating talk.

'Time you went to your room, young man,' she said.

'I'm waiting for everyone to go home,' I said. 'Then I'll help Sitaram tidy up. There's no cook, as you know.'

'Let him stay,' called Suresh from his bar stool. 'It's all part of his education. And he's old enough for a glass of beer. How old are you, sonny?'

'Sixteen,' I said.

'Well, enjoy yourself. It's later than you think.'

But I wasn't thinking of beer just then. I knew there were sausages in the fridge, and I had every intention of polishing them off as soon as all the guests had gone. I wanted to be a writer, but I had no intention of starving in a garret. However, all thoughts of food vanished when I looked across the room and saw Colonel Wilkie framed in the opposite doorway. He was staring at us through the glass. The glass door then opened of its own volition, and Colonel Wilkie stepped into the room. We all looked up, and Reggie said, 'Back again, Colonel? Still feeling thirsty?' But Colonel Wilkie ignored the jibe, and walked slowly across the room to the table where he had been sitting. This was close to where I was standing. He bent down and picked up his pipe from the table. He'd forgotten it when he'd left the bar-room. Shoving the pipe into his pocket, he turned and retraced his steps, leaving the room by the door from which he had entered.

'Well, I'm blowed,' said Krishan. 'I thought he was sleepwalking.'

'Never goes anywhere without his pipe,' said Suresh. 'A perfect example of single-mindedness.'

'Didn't say a word.'

'The pipe was all that mattered.'

'Like a favourite cricket bat,' said Krishan.

'Maybe I'll come back for mine when I'm dead.'

A silence fell upon the room. The mention of death had a sobering effect upon the small group. And come to think of it, Colonel Wilkie on his return to the bar-room had something of the zombie about him—the walking dead.

There was a commotion in the passageway, and my mother burst into the room, followed by the night-watchman.

'Colonel Wilkie's dead,' said my mother. 'He collapsed on his steps about half an hour ago.'

'But he was here five minutes ago,' said Krishan.

'No, sir,' said Gopal the watchman. 'I went home with him when he left here some time back. Madam said to keep an eye on him. When we got to his place, he began climbing his steps with some difficulty. I helped him to the top step, and then he collapsed. I dragged him into his room and then ran for Dr Bhist. He is there now.'

There was silence for a couple of minutes, and then Ruby said, 'We all saw him. Colonel Wilkie.'

'We saw his ghost,' Krishan murmured.

'He came for his pipe,' said Suresh quietly. 'I told you he wouldn't go anywhere without it.'

Colonel Wilkie was buried the next day, and we made sure his pipe was buried with him. We did not want him turning up from time to time, looking for it. It could be a bit unnerving for the customers.

In all the excitement I'd forgotten about the sausages, but decided they would keep until after the funeral.

All the regular barflies turned up for the funeral. H.H. was quite sloshed when she arrived and had to be extricated from an open grave into which she had slipped, the ground being soft and yielding after recent rain. She blamed secretary Simon for the mishap and called him an *ullu ka patha*—son of an owl—but he was quite used to such broadsides and took them in his stride. Was it love or loyalty or dependence that kept him in abeyance? Or was it, as some said, the prospect of becoming her heir? If so, he was paying a heavy price well in advance of such a prospect. Not everyone relishes being abused and kicked around in public by a half-crazed maharani.

When Colonel Wilkie's coffin was lowered into the grave, we all said 'Cheers!' He would have liked that. We then returned to Green's for an early opening of the bar. Alcoholics Unanimous held a subdued but not too melancholy meeting.

But bad news was in store for everyone. A day or two later, I heard the owner, our Sardarji, inform my mother that the hotel had been sold and that she'd have to leave at the end of the month. She'd been expecting something like this, and had already accepted a matron's job at one of the schools in the valley. As for me, I was to be packed off to England to my aunt's home in Jersey. The prospect did not thrill me, but I was more or less resigned to it. And there did not appear to be much future for me in Dehra.

Even before the month was out, workers had begun pulling down parts of the building. It was to be rebuilt as a cinema hall, and would show the latest hits from Bombay. It was even rumoured that Dilip Kumar, the biggest star of that era, would inaugurate the new cinema when it was ready to open.

The spirit and character of a building lasts only while the building lasts. Remove the roof-beams, pull down the walls, smash the stairways, and you are left with nothing but memories. Even the ghosts have nowhere to go.

An old hotel that once had a personality of its own was now dismantled with startling rapidity. It had gone up slowly, brick by brick; it came down like a house of cards. No treasures cascaded from its walls; no skeletons were discovered. In two or three days the demolishers had wiped out the past, removed Green's Hotel from the face of the earth so effectively that it might never have existed.

Searching through the ruins one day, I found a bottle-opener lying in the dust, and kept it as a souvenir.

The bar had been the only common factor in the lives of those disparate individuals who had come there so regularly—drawn to the place rather than to each other.

Now they went their different ways—Suresh Mathur to the Club, the Maharani to her card table and private bar, Krishan to a public school as a cricket coach, Reggie Bhowmik and Ruby to Darjeeling to make a documentary… Sitaram continued to work for my mother, so I had his company whenever he was free.

The cinema came up quite rapidly, but I had left for England before it opened. When I returned five years later, it was showing Madhubala and Guru Dutt in a romantic comedy, *Mr & Mrs 55.*

Then I moved to Delhi.

In recent years, some of the old single cinemas have been

closing down, giving way to multiplexes. The other day, passing through Dehra, I saw that 'our' cinema hall was being pulled down. 'What now?' I asked my taxi driver. 'A multiplex?' 'No, sir. A shopping mall!'

And such is progress.

I think I'm the only one around who is old enough to remember the old Green's Hotel, its dusty corridors, shabby bar-room, and oddball customers. All have gone. All forgotten! Not even footprints in the sands of time. But by putting down this memoir of an evening or two at that forgotten watering place, I think I have cheated Time just a little.

UPON AN OLD WALL DREAMING

It is time to confess that at least half my life has been spent in idleness. My old school would not be proud of me. Nor would my Aunt Muriel.

'You spend most of your time sitting on that wall, doing nothing,' scolded Aunt Muriel, when I was seven or eight. 'Are you *thinking* about something?'

'No, Aunt Muriel.'

'Are you *dreaming*?'

'I'm awake!'

'Then what on earth are you doing there?'

'Nothing, Aunt Muriel.'

'He'll come to no good,' she warned the world at large. 'He'll spend all his life sitting on walls, doing nothing.'

And how right she proved to be! Sometimes I bestir myself, and bang out a few sentences on my old typewriter, but most of the time I'm still sitting on that wall, preferably in the winter sunshine. Thinking? Not very deeply. Dreaming? But I've grown too old to dream. Meditation, perhaps. That's been fashionable for some time. But it isn't that either. Contemplation might come closer to the mark.

Was I born with a silver spoon in my mouth that I could afford to sit in the sun for hours, doing nothing? Far from it; I was born poor and remained poor, as far as worldly riches went. But one has to eat and pay the rent. And there have been others to feed too. So I have to admit that between long bouts of idleness there have been short bursts of creativity. My typewriter after more than thirty years of loyal service, has finally collapsed, proof enough that it has not lain idle all this time.

Sitting on walls, apparently doing nothing, has always been my favourite form of inactivity. But for these walls, and the many idle hours I have spent upon them, I would not have written even a fraction of the hundreds of stories, essays and other diversions that have been banged out on the typewriter over the years. It is not the walls themselves that set me off or give me ideas, but a personal view of the world that I receive from sitting there.

Creative idleness, you could call it. A receptivity to the world around me—the breeze, the warmth of the old stone, the lizard on the rock, a raindrop on a blade of grass—these and other impressions impinge upon me as I sit in that passive, benign condition that makes people smile tolerantly at me as they pass. 'Eccentric writer,' they remark to each other, as they drive on, hurrying in a heat of hope, towards the pot of gold at the end of their personal rainbows.

It's true that I am eccentric in many ways, and old walls bring out the essence of my eccentricity.

I do not have a garden wall. This shaky tumbledown house in the hills is perched directly above a motorable road, making me both accessible and vulnerable to casual callers of all kinds—inquisitive tourists, local busybodies, schoolgirls with their poems, hawkers selling candyfloss, itinerant sadhus, scrap merchants, potential Nobel Prize winners…

To escape them, and to set my thoughts in order, I walk a little way up the road, cross it, and sit down on a parapet wall overlooking the Woodstock spur. Here, partially shaded by an overhanging oak, I am usually left alone. I look suitably down and out, shabbily dressed, a complete nonentity—not the sort of person you would want to be seen talking to!

Stray dogs sometimes join me here. Having been a stray dog myself at various periods of my life, I can empathize with these friendly vagabonds of the road. Far more intelligent than your inbred Pom or Peke, they let me know by their silent companionship that they are on the same wavelength. They sport about on the road, but they do not yap at all and sundry.

Left to myself on the wall, I am soon in the throes of composing a story or poem. I do not write it down—that can be done later—I just work it out in my mind, memorize my words, so to speak, and keep them stored up for my next writing session.

Occasionally a car will stop, and someone I know will stick his head out and say, 'No work today, Mr Bond? How I envy you! Not a care in the world!'

I travel back in time some fifty years to Aunt Muriel asking me the same question. The years melt away, and I am a child again, sitting on the garden wall, doing nothing.

'Don't you get bored sitting there?' asks the latest passing motorist, who has one of those half-beards which are in vogue with TV news readers. 'What are you doing?'

'Nothing, Aunty,' I reply.

He gives me a long hard stare.

'You must be dreaming. Don't you recognize me?'

'Yes, Aunt Muriel.'

He shakes his head sadly, steps on the gas, and goes roaring up the hill in a cloud of dust.

'Poor old Bond,' he tells his friends over evening cocktails. 'Must be going round the bend. This morning he called me Aunty.'

THE KITEMAKER

There was but one tree in the street known as Gali Ram Nath—an ancient banyan that had grown through the cracks of an abandoned mosque—and little Ali's kite was caught in its branches. The boy, barefoot and clad only in a torn shirt, ran along the cobbled stones of the narrow street to where his grandfather sat nodding dreamily in the sunshine in their back courtyard.

'Grandfather,' shouted the boy. 'My kite has gone!'

The old man woke from his daydream with a start and, raising his head, displayed a beard that would have been white had it not been dyed red with mehendi leaves.

'Did the twine break?' he asked. 'I know that kite twine is not what it used to be.'

'No, Grandfather, the kite is stuck in the banyan tree.'

The old man chuckled. 'You have yet to learn how to fly a kite properly, my child. And I am too old to teach you, that's the pity of it. But you shall have another.'

He had just finished making a new kite from bamboo, paper and thin silk, and it lay in the sun, firming up. It was a pale pink kite, with a small green tail. The old man handed it to Ali, and the boy raised himself on his toes and kissed his grandfather's hollowed-out cheek.

'I will not lose this one,' he said. 'This kite will fly like a bird.' And he turned on his heels and skipped out of the courtyard.

The old man remained dreaming in the sun. His kite shop was gone, the premises long since sold to a junk dealer; but he still made kites, for his own amusement and for the benefit of his grandson, Ali. Not many people bought kites these days. Adults disdained them, and children preferred to spend their money at the cinema. Moreover, there were not many open spaces left for the flying of kites. The city had swallowed up the open grassland that had stretched from the old fort's walls to the river bank.

But the old man remembered a time when grown men flew kites, and great battles were fought, the kites swerving and swooping in the sky, tangling with each other until the string of one was severed. Then the defeated but liberated kite would float away into the blue unknown. There was a good deal of betting, and money frequently changed hands.

Kite flying was then the sport of kings, and the old man remembered how the Nawab himself would come down to the riverside with his retinue to participate in this noble pastime. There was time, then, to spend an idle hour with a gay, dancing strip of paper. Now everyone hurried, in a heat of hope, and delicate things like kites and daydreams were trampled underfoot.

He, Mehmood the kitemaker, had in the prime of his life been well known throughout the city. Some of his more elaborate kites once sold for as much as three or four rupees each.

At the request of the Nawab he had once made a very special kind of kite, unlike any that had been seen in the district. It consisted of a series of small, very light paper disks trailing on a thin bamboo frame. To the end of each disk he fixed a sprig of grass, forming a balance on both sides. The surface of the foremost disk was slightly convex, and a fantastic face was painted on it, having two eyes made of small mirrors. The disks, decreasing in size from head to tail, assumed an undulatory form and gave the kite the appearance of a crawling serpent. It required great skill to raise this cumbersome device from the ground, and only Mehmood could manage it.

Everyone had heard of the 'Dragon Kite' that Mehmood had built, and word went round that it possessed supernatural powers. A large crowd assembled in the open to watch its first public launching in the presence of the Nawab.

At the first attempt it refused to leave the ground. The disks made a plaintive, protesting sound, and the sun was trapped in the little mirrors, making the kite a living, complaining creature. Then the wind came from the right direction, and the Dragon Kite soared into the sky, wriggling its way higher and higher, the sun still glinting in its devil eyes. And when it went very high, it pulled fiercely at the twine, and Mehmood's young sons had to help him with the reel. Still the kite pulled, determined to be free, to break loose, to live a life of its own. And eventually it did so.

The twine snapped, the kite leaped away towards the sun, sailing on heavenward until it was lost to view. It was never found again, and Mehmood wondered afterwards if he had made too vivid, too living a thing of the great kite. He did not make another like it. Instead he presented to the Nawab a musical kite, one that made a sound like a violin when it rose into the air.

Those were more leisurely, more spacious days. But the Nawab had died years ago, and his descendants were almost as poor as Mehmood himself. Kitemakers, like poets, once had their patrons; but now no one knew Mehmood, simply because there were too many people in the Gali, and they could not be bothered with their neighbours.

When Mehmood was younger and had fallen sick, everyone in the neighbourhood had come to ask after his health, but now, when his days were drawing to a close, no one visited him. Most of his old friends were dead and his sons had grown up: one was working in a local garage and the other, who was in Pakistan at the time of the Partition, had not been able to rejoin his relatives.

The children who had bought kites from him ten years ago were now grown men, struggling for a living; they did not have time for the old man and his memories. They had grown up in a swiftly changing and competitive world, and they looked at the old kitemaker and the banyan tree with the same indifference.

Both were taken for granted—permanent fixtures that were of no concern to the raucous, sweating mass of humanity that surrounded them. No longer did people gather under the banyan tree to discuss their problems and their plans; only in the summer months did a few seek shelter from the fierce sun.

But there was the boy, his grandson. It was good that Mehmood's son worked close by, for it gladdened the old man's heart to watch the small boy at play in the winter sunshine, growing under his eyes like a young and well-nourished sapling putting forth new leaves each day. There is a great affinity between trees and men. We grow at much the same pace, if we are not hurt or starved or cut down. In our youth we are resplendent creatures, and in our declining years we stoop a little, we remember, we stretch our brittle limbs in the sun, and then, with a sigh, we shed our last leaves.

Mehmood was like the banyan, his hands gnarled and twisted like the roots of the ancient tree. Ali was like the young mimosa planted at the end of the courtyard. In two years, both he and the tree would acquire the strength and confidence of their early youth.

The voices in the street grew fainter, and Mehmood wondered if he was going to fall asleep and dream, as he so often did, of a kite so beautiful and powerful that it would resemble the great white bird of the Hindus—Garuda, God

Vishnu's famous steed. He would like to make a wonderful new kite for little Ali. He had nothing else to leave the boy.

He heard Ali's voice in the distance, but did not realize that the boy was calling him. The voice seemed to come from very far away.

Ali was at the courtyard door, asking if his mother had as yet returned from the bazaar. When Mehmood did not answer, the boy came forward repeating his question. The sunlight was slanting across the old man's head, and a small white butterfly rested on his flowing beard. Mehmood was silent; and when Ali put his small brown hand on the old man's shoulder, he met with no response. The boy heard a faint sound, like the rubbing of marbles in his pocket.

Suddenly afraid, Ali turned and moved to the door, and then ran down the street shouting for his mother. The butterfly left the old man's beard and flew to the mimosa tree, and a sudden gust of wind caught the torn kite and lifted it in the air, carrying it far above the struggling city into the blind blue sky.

IN GRANDFATHER'S GARDEN

Though the house and grounds of our home in Dehra were Grandfather's domain—where he kept an odd assortment of pets—the magnificent old banyan tree was mine, chiefly because Grandfather, at the age of sixty-five, could no longer climb it. Grandmother used to tease him about this, and would speak of a certain Countess of Desmond, an Englishwoman who lived to the age of 117, and would have lived longer if she hadn't fallen while climbing an apple tree. The spreading branches of the banyan tree, which curved to the ground and took root again, forming a maze of arches, gave me endless pleasure. The tree was older than the house, older than Grandfather, as old as the town of Dehra, nestling in a valley at the foot of the Himalayas.

My first friend and familiar was a small grey squirrel. Arching his back and sniffing into the air, he seemed at first to resent my invasion of his privacy. But when he found that I did not arm myself with a catapult or air-gun, he became friendlier. And when I started leaving him pieces of cake and biscuit, he grew bolder, and finally became familiar enough to take food from my hands.

Before long he was delving into my pockets and helping himself to whatever he could find. He was a very young squirrel, and his friends and relatives probably thought him headstrong and foolish for trusting a human.

In the spring, when the banyan tree was full of small red figs, birds of all kinds would flock into its branches, the red-bottomed bulbul, cheerful and greedy, gossiping rosy pastors, and parrots and crows, squabbling with each other all the time. During the fig season, the banyan tree was the noisiest place on the road.

Halfway up the tree I had built a small platform on which I would often spend the afternoons when it wasn't too hot. I could read there, propping myself up against the bole of the tree with the cushions taken from the drawing room. *Treasure Island*, Huck Finn, the Mowgli stories, and detective novels made up my bag of very mixed reading.

When I didn't want to read, I could look down through the banyan leaves at the world below, at Grandmother hanging up or taking down the washing, at the cook quarrelling with a fruit vendor, or at Grandfather grumbling at the hardy Indian marigold, which insisted on springing up all over his very English garden. Usually nothing very exciting happened while I was in the banyan tree, but on one particular afternoon I had enough excitement to last me through the summer.

That was the time I saw a mongoose and a cobra fight to death in the garden, while I sat directly above them in the banyan tree.

It was an April afternoon. The warm breezes of approaching summer had sent everyone, including Grandfather, indoors. I was feeling drowsy myself and was wondering if I should go to the pond behind the house for a swim, when I saw a huge black cobra gliding out of a clump of cacti and making for some cooler part of the garden. At the same time a mongoose (whom I had often seen) emerged from the bushes and went straight for the cobra.

In a clearing beneath the tree, in bright sunshine, they came face to face.

The cobra knew only too well that the grey mongoose, three feet long, was a superb fighter, clever and aggressive. But the cobra was a skilful and experienced fighter, too. He could move swiftly and strike with the speed of light, and the sacs behind his long, sharp fangs were full of deadly venom.

It was to be a battle of champions.

Hissing defiance, his forked tongue darting in and out, the cobra raised three of his six feet off the ground, and spread his broad, spectacled hood. The mongoose bushed his tail. The long hair on his spine stood up (in the past, the very thickness of his hair had saved him from bites that would have been fatal to others).

Though the combatants were unaware of my presence in the banyan tree, they soon became aware of the arrival of two other spectators. One was a mynah, and the other a jungle crow (not the wily urban crow). They had seen these preparations for battle, and had settled on the cactus to watch the outcome. Had they been content only to watch, all would have been well with both of them.

The cobra stood on the defensive, swaying slowly from side to side, trying to mesmerize the mongoose into making a false move. The mongoose knew the power of his opponent's glassy, twinkling eyes, and refused to meet them. Instead, he fixed his gaze at a point just below the cobra's hood, and opened the attack.

Moving forward quickly until he was just within the cobra's reach, he made a feint to one side. Immediately the cobra struck. His great hood came down so swiftly that I thought nothing could save the mongoose. But the little fellow jumped neatly to one side, and darted in as swiftly as the cobra, biting the snake on the back and darting away again out of reach.

The moment the cobra struck, the crow and the mynah hurled themselves at him, only to collide heavily in mid-air. Shrieking at each other, they returned to the cactus plant.

A few drops of blood glistened on the cobra's back.

The cobra struck again and missed. Again the mongoose sprang aside, jumped in and bit. Again the birds dived at the snake, bumped into each other instead, and returned shrieking to the safety of the cactus.

The third round followed the same course as the first but with one dramatic difference. The crow and the mynah, still determined to take part in the proceedings, dived at the cobra, but this time they missed each other as well as their mark. The mynah flew on and reached its perch, but the crow tried to pull up in mid-air and turn back. In the second that it took him to do this, the cobra whipped his head back and struck with great force, his snout thudding against the crow's body.

I saw the bird flung nearly twenty feet across the garden, where, after fluttering about for a while, it lay still. The mynah remained on the cactus plant, and when the snake and the mongoose returned to the fray, it very wisely refrained from interfering again!

The cobra was weakening, and the mongoose, walking fearlessly up to it, raised himself on his short legs, and with a lightning snap had the big snake by the snout. The cobra writhed and lashed about in a frightening manner, and even coiled itself about the mongoose, but all to no avail. The little fellow hung grimly on, until the snake had ceased to struggle. He then smeared along its quivering length, gripping it round the hood, and dragging it into the bushes.

The mynah dropped cautiously to the ground, hopped about, peered into the bushes from a safe distance, and then, with a shrill cry of congratulation, flew away.

When I had also made a cautious descent from the tree and returned to the house, I told Grandfather of the fight I had seen. He was pleased that the mongoose had won. He had encouraged it to live in the garden, to keep away the snakes, and fed it regularly with scraps from the kitchen. He had never tried taming it, because a wild mongoose was more useful than a domesticated one.

From the banyan tree I often saw the mongoose patrolling the four corners of the garden, and once I saw him with an egg in his mouth and knew he had been in the poultry house; but he hadn't harmed the birds, and I knew Grandmother would forgive him for stealing as long as he kept the snakes away.

The banyan tree was also the setting for what we were to call the Strange Case of the Grey Squirrel and the White Rat.

The white rat was Grandfather's—he had bought it from the bazaar for four annas—but I would often take it with me into the banyan tree, where it soon struck up a friendship with one of the squirrels. They would go off together on little excursions among the roots and branches of the old tree.

Then the squirrel started building a nest. At first she tried building it in my pockets, and when I went indoors and changed my clothes I would find straw and grass falling out. Then one day Grandmother's knitting was missing. We hunted for it everywhere but without success.

Next day I saw something glinting in the hole in the banyan tree and, going up to investigate, saw that it was the end of Grandmother's steel knitting needle. On looking further, I discovered that the hole was crammed with knitting. And amongst the wool were three baby squirrels—all of them white!

Grandfather had never seen white squirrels before, and we gazed at them in wonder. We were puzzled for some time, but when I mentioned the white rat's frequent visits to the tree, Grandfather told me that the rat must be the father. Rats and squirrels were related to each other, he said, and so it was quite possible for them to have offspring—in this case, white squirrels!

THOSE SIMPLE THINGS

It's the *simple* things in life that keep us from going crazy.

Like that pigeon in the skylight in the New Delhi Nursing Home where I was incarcerated for two or three days. Even worse than the illness that had brought me there were the series of tests that the doctors insisted I had to go through—gastroscopies, endoscopies, X-rays, blood tests, urine tests, probes into any orifice they could find, and at the end of it all a nice fat bill designed to give me a heart attack.

The only thing that prevented me from running into the street, shouting for help, was that pigeon in the skylight. It sheltered there at various times during the day, and its gentle cooing soothed my nerves and kept me in touch with the normal world outside. I owe my sanity to that pigeon.

Which reminds me of the mouse who shared my little bed-sitting room in London, when I was just seventeen and all on my own. Those early months in London were lonely times for a shy young man going to work during the day and coming back to a cold, damp, empty room late in the evening. In the morning I would make myself a hurried breakfast, and at night I'd make myself a cheese or ham sandwich. This was when I noticed the little mouse peeping out at me from behind the books I had piled up on the floor, there being no bookshelf. I threw some crumbs in his direction, and he was soon making a meal of them and a piece of cheese. After that, he would present himself before me every evening, and the room was no longer as empty and lonely as when I had first moved in.

He was a smart little mouse and sometimes he would speak to me—sharp little squeaks to remind me it was dinner time.

Months later, when I moved to another part of London, I had to leave him behind—I did not want to deprive him of friends and family—but it was a fat little mouse I left behind.

During my three years in London I must have lived in at least half a dozen different lodging houses, and the rooms were usually dull and depressing. One had a window looking out on a railway track; another provided me with a great view of a cemetery. To spend my day off looking down upon hundreds of graves was hardly uplifting, even if some of the tombstones were beautifully sculpted. No wonder I spent my evenings watching old Marx Brothers films at the Everyman Cinema nearby.

Living in small rooms for the greater part of my life, I have always felt the need for small, familiar objects that become a part of me, even if sometimes I forget to say hello to them. A glass paperweight, a laughing Buddha, an old horseshoe, a print of Hokusai's *Great Wave*, a suitcase that has seen better days, an old school tie (never worn, but there all the same), a gramophone record (can't play it now, but when I look at it, the song comes back to me), a potted fern, an old address book… Where have they gone, those old familiar faces? Not one address is relevant today (after some forty years), but I keep it all the same.

I turn to a page at the end, and discover why I have kept it all these years. It holds a secret, scribbled note to an early love:

> 'I did not sleep last night, for you had kissed me. You held my hand and put it to your cheek and to your breasts. And I had closed your eyes and kissed them, and taken

your face in my hands and touched your lips with mine. And then, my darling, I stumbled into the light like a man intoxicated, and did not know what people were saying or doing…'

Gosh! How romantic I was at thirty! And reading that little entry, I feel like going out and falling in love again. But will anyone fall in love with an old man of seventy-five?

Yes! There's a little mouse in my room.

COMING HOME TO DEHRA

The faint queasiness I always feel towards the end of a journey probably has its origin in that first homecoming after my father's death.

It was the winter of 1944—yes, a long time ago—and the train was running through the thick sal forests near Dehra, bringing me at every click of the rails nearer to the mother I hadn't seen for four years and the stepfather I had seen just once or twice before my parents were divorced.

I was eleven and I was coming home to Dehra.

Three years earlier, after the separation, I had gone to live with my father. We were very happy together. He was serving in the RAF, at New Delhi, and we lived in a large tent somewhere near Humayun's Tomb. The area is now a very busy part of urban Delhi, but in those days it was still a wilderness of scrub jungle where black buck and nilgai roamed freely. We took long walks together, exploring the ruins of old tombs and forts; went to the pictures (George Formby comedies were special favourites of mine); collected stamps; bought books (my father had taught me to read and write before I started going to school); and made plans for going to England when the war was over.

Six months of bliss, even though it was summer and there weren't any fans, only a thick khus reed curtain that had to be splashed with water every hour by a bhisti who did the rounds of similar tents with his goat-skin water bag. I remember the tender refreshing fragrance of the khus, and also the smell of damp earth outside, where the water had spilt.

A happy time. But it had to end. My father's periodic bouts of malarial fever resulted in his having to enter hospital for a week. The bhisti's small son came to stay with me at night, and during the day I took my meals with an Anglo-Indian family across the road.

I would have been quite happy to continue with this arrangement whenever my father was absent, but someone at air headquarters must have advised him to put me in a boarding school.

Reluctantly he came to the decision that this would be the best thing—'until the war is over'—and in the June of 1943 he took me to Shimla, where I was incarcerated in a preparatory school for boys.

This is not the story of my life at boarding school. It might easily have been a public school in England; it did in fact pride itself on being the 'Eton of the East'. The traditions—such as ragging and flogging, compulsory games and chapel attendance, prefects larger than life, and honour boards for everything from school captaincy to choir membership—had all apparently been borrowed from *Tom Brown's Schooldays.*

My father wrote to me regularly, and his letters were the things I looked forward to more than anything else. I went to him for the winter holidays, and the following summer he came to Shimla during my mid-term break and took me out for the duration of the holidays. We stayed in a hotel called Craig-Dhu, on a spur north of Jacko Hill. It was an idyllic week; long walks; stories about phantom rickshaws; ice creams in the sun; browsings in bookshops; more plans: 'We will go to England next year.'

School seemed a stupid and heartless place after my father

had gone away. He had been transferred to Calcutta and he wasn't keeping well there. Malaria again. And then jaundice. But his last letter sounded quite cheerful. He'd been selling part of his valuable stamp collection so as to have enough money for the fares to England.

One day my class teacher sent for me.

'I want to talk to you, Bond,' he said. 'Let's go for a walk.'

I knew immediately that something was wrong.

We took the path that went through the deodar forest, past Council Rock where scout meetings were held. As soon as my unfortunate teacher (no doubt cursing the headmaster for having given him this unpleasant task) started on the theme of 'God wanting your father in a higher and better place,' as though there could be any better place than Jacko Hill in mid-summer, I knew my father was dead, and burst into tears.

They let me stay in the school hospital for a few days until I felt better. The headmaster visited me there and took away the pile of my father's letters that I'd kept beside me.

'Your father's letters. You might lose them. Why not leave them with me? Then at the end of the year, before you go home, you can come and collect them.'

Unwillingly I gave him the letters. He told me he'd heard from my mother that I would be going home to her at the end of the year. He seemed surprised that I evinced no interest in this prospect.

At the end of the year, the day before school closed, I went to the headmaster's office and asked for my letters.

'What letters?' he said. His desk was piled with papers and correspondence, and he was irritated by my interruption.

'My father's letters,' I explained. 'I gave them to you to keep for me, sir—when he died…'

'Letters. Are you sure you gave them to me?'

He grew more irritated. 'You must be mistaken, Bond. Why should I want to keep your father's letters?'

'I don't know, sir. You said I could collect them before going home.'

'Look, I don't remember any letters and I'm very busy just now, so run along. I'm sure you're mistaken, but if I find your letters, I'll send them to you.'

I don't suppose he meant to be unkind, but he was the first man who aroused in me feelings of hate...

As the train drew into Dehra, I looked out of the window to see if there was anyone on the platform waiting to receive me. The station was crowded enough, as most railway stations are in India, with overloaded travellers, shouting coolies, stray dogs, stray stationmasters... Pandemonium broke loose as the train came to a halt and people debauched from the carriages. I was thrust on the platform with my tin trunk and small attaché case. I sat on the trunk and waited for someone to find me.

Slowly the crowd melted away. I was left with one elderly coolie who was too feeble to carry heavy luggage and had decided that my trunk was just the right size and weight for his head and shoulders. I waited another ten minutes, but no representative of my mother or stepfather appeared. I permitted the coolie to lead me out of the station to the tonga stand.

Those were the days when everyone, including high-ranking officials, went about in tongas. Dehra had just one taxi. I was quite happy sitting beside a rather smelly, paan-spitting tonga driver, while his weary, underfed pony clip-clopped along the quiet tree-lined roads.

Dehra was always a good place for trees. The valley soil is very fertile, the rainfall fairly heavy; almost everything grows there, if given the chance. The roads were lined with neem and mango trees, eucalyptus, Persian lilac, jacaranda, amaltas (laburnum) and many others. In the gardens of the bungalows were mangoes, litchis and guavas; sometimes jackfruit and papaya. I did not notice all these trees at once; I came to know them as time passed.

The tonga first took me to my grandmother's house. I was under the impression that my mother still lived there.

A lovely, comfortable bungalow that spread itself about the grounds in an easy going, old-fashioned way. There was even smoke coming from the chimneys, reminding me of the smoke from my grandfather's pipe. When I was eight, I had spent several months there with my grandparents. In retrospect it had been an idyllic interlude. But Grandfather was dead. Grandmother lived alone.

White-haired, but still broad in the face and even broader behind, she was astonished to see me getting down from the tonga.

'Didn't anyone meet you at the station?' she asked.

I shook my head. Grandmother said: 'Your mother doesn't live here any more. You can come in and wait, but she may be worried about you, so I'd better take you to her place. Come on, help me up into the tonga... I might have known it would be a white horse. It always makes me nervous sitting in a tonga behind a white horse.'

'Why, Granny?'

'I don't know, I suppose white horses are nervous, too. Anyway, they are always trying to topple me out. Not so fast, driver!' she called out, as the tonga man cracked his whip and the pony changed from a slow shuffle to a brisk trot.

It took us about twenty-five minutes to reach my stepfather's house which was in the Dalanwala area, not far from the dry bed of the seasonal Rispana river. My grandmother, seeing that I was in need of moral support, got down with me, while the tonga driver carried my bedding roll and tin trunk on to the veranda.

The front door was bolted from inside. We had to knock on it repeatedly and call out before it was opened by a servant who did not look pleased at being disturbed. When he saw my grandmother he gave her a deferential salaam, then gazed at me with open curiosity.

'Where's the memsahib?' asked Grandmother.

'Out,' said the servant.

'I can see that but where have they gone?'

'They went yesterday to Motichur, for shikar. They will be back this evening.'

Grandmother looked upset, but motioned to the servant to bring in my things. 'Weren't they expecting the boy?' she asked. 'Yes,' he said looking at me again. 'But they said he would be arriving tomorrow.'

'They'd forgotten the date,' said Grandmother in a huff. 'Anyway, you can unpack and have a wash and change your clothes.'

Turning to the servant, she asked, 'Is there any lunch?'

'I will make lunch,' he said. He was staring at me again, and I felt uneasy with his eyes on me. He was tall and swarthy, with oily, jet-back hair and a thick moustache. A heavy scar ran down his left cheek, giving him a rather sinister appearance. He wore a torn shirt and dirty pyjamas. His broad, heavy feet were wet. They left marks on the uncarpeted floor.

A baby was crying in the next room, and presently a woman (who turned out to be the cook's wife) appeared in the doorway, jogging the child in her arms.

'They've left the baby behind, too,' said Grandmother, becoming more and more irate. 'He is your young brother. Only six months old.' I hadn't been told anything about a younger brother. The discovery that I had one came as something of a shock. I wasn't prepared for a baby brother, least of all a baby half-brother. I examined the child without much enthusiasm. He looked healthy enough and he cried with gusto.

'He's a beautiful baby,' said Grandmother. 'Well, I've got work to do. The servants will look after you. You can come and see me in a day or two. You've grown since I last saw you. And you're getting pimples.'

This reference to my appearance did not displease me as Grandmother never indulged in praise. For her to have observed my pimples indicated that she was fond of me.

The tonga driver was waiting for her. 'I suppose I'll have to use the same tonga,' she said. 'Whenever I need a tonga, they disappear, except for the ones with white ponies. When your mother gets back, tell her I want to see her. Shikar, indeed. An infant to look after, and they've gone shooting.'

Grandmother settled herself in the tonga, nodded in response to the cook's salaam, and took a tight grip of the armrests of her seat. The driver flourished his whip and the pony set off at the same listless, unhurried trot, while my grandmother, feeling quite certain that she was going to be hurtled to her doom by a wild white pony, set her teeth and clung tenaciously to the tonga seat. I was sorry to see her go.

My mother and stepfather returned in the evening from their hunting trip with a pheasant which was duly handed over to the cook, whose name was Mangal Singh. My mother gave me a perfunctory kiss. I think she was pleased to see me, but I was accustomed to a more intimate caress from my father, and the strange reception I had received made me realize the extent of my loss. Boarding school life had been routine. Going home was something that I had always looked forward to. But going home had meant my father, and now he had vanished and I was left quite desolate.

I suppose if one is present when a loved one dies, or sees him dead and laid out and later buried, one is convinced of the finality of the thing and finds it easier to adapt to the changed circumstances. But when you hear of a death, a father's death, and have only the faintest idea of the manner of his dying, it is rather a lot for the imagination to cope with—especially when the imagination is a small boy's. There being no tangible evidence of my father's death, it was, for me, not a death but a vanishing. And although this enabled me to remember him as a living, smiling, breathing person, it meant that I was not wholly reconciled to his death, and subconsciously expected him to turn up (as he often did, when I most needed him) and deliver me from any unpleasant situation.

My stepfather barely noticed me. The first thing he did on coming into the house was to pour himself a whisky and soda. My mother, after inspecting the baby, did likewise. I was left to unpack and settle in my room.

I was fortunate in having my own room. I was as desirous of my own privacy as much as my mother and stepfather were desirous of theirs. My stepfather, a local businessman, was ready to put up with me provided I did not get in the way. And, in a different way, I was ready to put up with him, provided he left me alone. I was even willing that my mother should leave me alone. There was a big window to my room, and I opened it to the evening breeze, and gazed out on to the garden, a rather unkempt place where marigolds and a sort of wild blue everlasting grew rampant among the litchi trees.

THE POSTMAN KNOCKS

As a freelance writer, most of my adult life has revolved around the coming of the postman. 'A cheque in the mail,' is something that every struggling writer looks forward to. It might, of course, arrive by courier, or it might not come at all. But for the most part, the acceptances and rejections of my writing life, along with editorial correspondence, readers' letters, page proofs and author's copies—how welcome they are!—come through the post.

The postman has always played a very real and important part in my life, and continues to do so. He climbs my twenty-one steps every afternoon, knocks loudly on my door—three raps, so that I know it's him and not some inquisitive tourist—and gives me my registered mail or speed-post with a smile and a bit of local gossip. The gossip is important. I like to know what's happening in the bazaar—who's getting married, who's standing for election, who ran away with the headmaster's wife, and whose funeral procession is passing by. He deserves a bonus for this sort of information.

The courier boy, by contrast, shouts to me from the road below and I have to go down to him. He's mortally afraid of dogs and there are three in the building. My postman isn't bothered by dogs. He comes in all weathers, and he comes on foot except when someone gives him a lift. He turns up when it's snowing, or when it's raining cats and dogs, or when there's a heat wave, and he's quite philosophical about it all. He meets all kinds of people. He has seen joy and sorrow in the homes he visits. He knows something about life. If he wasn't a philosopher to begin with, he will certainly be one by the time he retires.

Of course, not all postmen are paragons of virtue. A few years ago, we had a postman who never got further than the country liquor shop in the bazaar. The mail would pile up there for days, until he sobered up and condescended to deliver it. In due course, he was banished to another route, where there were no liquor shops.

We take the postman for granted today, but there was a time, over a hundred years ago, when the carrying of the mails was a hazardous venture, and the mail-runner, or *hirkara* as he was called, had to be armed with sword or spear. Letters were carried in leather wallets on the backs of runners, who were changed at stages of eight miles. At night, the runners were accompanied by torch-bearers—in wilder parts, by drummers called *dug-dugi wallas*—to frighten away wild animals.

The tiger population was considerable at the time, and tigers were a real threat to travellers or anyone who ventured far from their town or village. Mail-runners often fell victim to man-eating tigers. The mail-runners (most of them tribals) were armed with bows and arrows, but these were seldom effective.

In the Hazaribagh district (through which the mail had to be carried, on its way from Calcutta to Allahabad) there appears to have been a concentration of man-eating tigers. There were four passes through this district, and the tigers had them well covered. Williamson, writing in 1810, tells us that the passes were so infested with tigers that the roads were almost impassable. 'Day after day, for nearly a fortnight, some of the dak people were carried off at one or other of these passes.'

In spite of these hazards, a letter sent by dak runner used to take twelve days to reach Meerut from Calcutta. It takes about the same time today, unless you use speed-post.

At up country stations, the collector of Land Revenue was the Postmaster. He was given a small postal establishment, consisting of a *munshi,* a *matsaddi* or sorter, and thirty or for, runners whose pay, in 1804, was five rupees a month. The maintenance of the dak cost the government (i.e., the East India Company) twenty-five rupees a month for each stage of eight miles. Postage stamps were introduced in 1854.

My father was an enthusiastic philatelist, and when I was a small boy I could sit and watch him pore over his stamp collection, which included several early and valuable Indian issues. He would grumble at the very dark and smudgy postmarks which obliterated most of Queen Victoria's profile from the stamps. This was due to the composition of the ink used for cancelling the earlier stamps. It was composed of two parts lamp-black, four parts linseed oil and three and a half of vinegar.

Letter-distributing peons, or postmen, were always smartly turned out: 'A red turban, a light green chapkan, a small leather belt over the breast and right shoulder, with a chaprass attached showing the peon's number and having the words "Post Office Peon" in English and in two vernaculars, and a bell suspended by a leather strap from the left shoulder.'

Today's postmen are more casual in their attire, although I believe they are still entitled to uniforms. The general public doesn't care how they are dressed, as long as they turn up with those letters containing rakhis or money orders from soldiers, peons and husbands. This is where the postman still scores over the fax and email.

To return to our mail-runners, they were eventually replaced by the *dak-ghari*, the equivalent of the English 'coach and pair'—which gradually established itself throughout the country.

A survivor into the 1940s, my great-aunt Lillian recalled that in the late nineteenth century, before the coming of the railway, the only way of getting to Dehradun was by the dak-ghari or Night Mail. Dak-ghari ponies were difficult animals, she told me—'always attempting to turn around and get into the carriage with the passengers!' But once they started there was no stopping them. It was a gallop all the way to the first stage, where the ponies were changed to the accompaniment of a bugle blown by the coachman, in true Dickensian fashion.

The journey through the Siwaliks really began—as it still does—through the Mohand Pass. The ascent starts with a gradual gradient which increases as the road becomes more steep and winding. At this stage of the journey, drums were beaten (if it was day) and torches lit (if it was night) because sometimes wild elephants resented the approach of the dak-ghari and, trumpeting a challenge, would throw the ponies into confusion and panic, and send them racing back to the plains.

After 1900, great-aunt Lillian used the train. But the main bus from Saharanpur to Mussoorie still uses the old route through the Siwaliks. And if you are lucky, you may see a herd of wild elephants crossing the road on its way to the Ganga.

And even today, in remote parts of the country, in isolated hill areas where there are no motorable roads, the mail is carried on foot, the postman often covering five or six miles every day. He never runs, true, and he might sometimes stop for a glass of tea and a game of cards en-route, but he is a reminder of those early pioneers of the postal system, the mail-runners of India.

◆

Let me not cavil at my unexpected visitors. Sometimes they turn out to be very nice people—like the gentleman from Pune who brought me a bottle of whisky and then sat down and drank most of it himself.

BREAKFAST TIME

I like a good sausage, I do;
It's a dish for the chosen and few.
Oh, for sausage and mash,
And of mustard a dash,
And an egg nicely fried—maybe two?
At breakfast or lunch, or at dinner,
The sausage is always a winner;
If you want a good spread,
Go for sausage on bread,
And forget all your vows to be slimmer.

'In Praise of the Sausage'
(Written for Victor and Maya Banerjee,
who excel at making sausage breakfasts.)

There is something to be said for breakfast.

If you take an early morning walk down Landour Bazaar, you might be fortunate enough to see a very large cow standing in the foyer of a hotel, munching on a succulent cabbage or cauliflower. The owner of the hotel has a soft spot for this particular cow, and invites it in for breakfast every morning. Having had its fill, the cow—very well-behaved—backs out of the shop and makes way for paying customers.

I am not one of them. I prefer to have my breakfast at home—a fried egg, two or three buttered toasts, a bit of bacon if I'm lucky, otherwise some fish pickle from the south, followed by a cup of strong coffee—and I'm a happy man and can take the rest of the day in my stride.

I don't think I have ever written a good story without a good breakfast. There are, of course, writers who do not eat before noon. Both they and their prose have a lean and hungry look. Dickens was good at describing breakfasts and dinners—especially Christmas repasts—and many of his most rounded characters were good-natured people who were fond of their food and drink—Mr Pickwick, the Cheeryble brothers, Mr Weller senior, Captain Cuttle—as opposed to the half-starved characters in the works of some other Victorian writers. And remember, Dickens had an impoverished childhood. So I took it as a compliment when a little girl came up to me the other day and said, 'Sir, you're Mr Pickwick!'

As a young man, I had a lean and hungry look. After all, I was often hungry. Now if I look like Pickwick, I take it as an achievement.

And all those breakfasts had something to do with it.

It's not only cows and early-to-rise writers who enjoy a good breakfast. Last summer, Colonel Solomon was out taking his pet Labrador for an early morning walk near Lal Tibba when a leopard sprang out of a thicket, seized the dog and made off with it down the hillside. The dog did not even have time to yelp. Nor did the Colonel. Suffering from shock, he left Landour the next day and has yet to return.

Another leopard—this time at the other end of Mussoorie—entered the Savoy hotel at dawn, and finding nothing in the kitchen except chicken's feathers, moved on to the billiard room and there vented its frustration on the cloth of the billiard table, clawing it to shreds. The leopard was seen in various parts of the hotel before it made off in the direction of the Ladies' Block.

Just a hungry leopard in search of a meal. But three days later, Nandu Jauhar, the owner of the Savoy, found himself short of a lady housekeeper. Had she eloped with the laundryman, or had she become a good breakfast for the leopard? We do not know till this day.

English breakfasts, unlike continental breakfasts, are best enjoyed in India where you don't have to rush off to catch a bus or a train or get to your office in time. You can linger over your scrambled egg and marmalade on toast. What would breakfast be without some honey or marmalade? You can have an excellent English breakfast at the India International Centre, where I have spent many pleasant reflective mornings... And a super breakfast at the Raj Mahal Hotel in Jaipur. But some hotels give very inferior breakfasts, and I am afraid that certain Mussoorie establishments are great offenders, specializing in singed omelettes and burnt toasts.

Many people are under the erroneous impression that the days of the British Raj were synonymous with huge meals and unlimited food and drink. This may have been the case in the days of the East India Company, but was far from being so during the last decade of British rule. Those final years coincided with World War II, when food rationing was in force. At my boarding school in Shimla, omelettes were made from powdered eggs, and the contents of the occasional sausage were very mysterious—so much so, that we called our sausages 'sweet mysteries of life!' after a popular Nelson Eddy song.

Things were not much better at home. Just porridge (no eggs!) bread and jam (no butter!), and tea with *ghur* instead of refined sugar. The *ghur* was, of course, much healthier than sugar.

Breakfasts are better now, at least for those who can afford them. The jam is better than it used to be. So is the bread. And I can enjoy a fried egg, or even two, without feeling guilty about it. But good omelettes are still hard to come by. They shouldn't be made in a hurried or slapdash manner. Some thought has to go into an omelette. And a little love too. It's like writing a book—done much better with some feeling!

THE LAST WALNUT

It was nice to have a walnut tree just outside the window. It was a tree for all seasons. In winter, the branches were bare; but they were smooth, straight and round like the arms of an apsara. In spring, each branch produced a hard bright spear of new leaf. By midsummer the entire tree was in leaf, and towards the end of the monsoon the walnuts, encased in their green jackets, had reached their full maturity.

Then the jackets began to split, revealing the hard brown shell of the walnuts. Inside the shell was the nut itself. Look closely at the nut, and you will notice that it is shaped rather like the human brain. No wonder the ancients prescribed walnuts for headaches.

Every year the tree made us a gift of a basket of walnuts. But last year the walnuts were disappearing one by one, and I was at a loss to know who had been taking them.

Could it have been Bijju, the milkman's son? He was an inveterate tree-climber. But he was usually found up oak trees, gathering fodder for his cows. He told me that the cows did not care for walnuts. He admitted that they had relished my dahlias which they had eaten the previous week, but he denied having given them any walnuts.

Later, I found a fat langur sitting in the walnut tree. I watched him for some time to see if he was going to help himself to the nuts, but he was only sunning himself. When he thought I wasn't looking, he came down and ate the geraniums; but he did not take any walnuts.

It wasn't the woodpecker. He was out there every day, knocking furiously against the bark of the tree, trying to prise an insect out of a narrow crack. He was strictly non-vegetarian and none the worse for it.

The walnuts had been disappearing early in the morning, while I was still in bed. So one morning I surprised everyone, including myself, by getting up before sunrise. I was just in time to catch the culprit climbing down the walnut tree.

She was an old woman, who sometimes came to cut grass on the hillside. Her face was as wrinkled as the walnuts she had been pinching. But in spite of her age, her arms and legs were sturdy. When she saw me, she was as swift as a civet cat in getting out of the tree.

'Only two,' she said with a giggle, offering them to me on her outstretched palm.

I took one of the walnuts; and thus encouraged, she climbed back into the tree and helped herself to the remaining walnuts. It was impossible to object. I was taken up in admiring her agility in the tree, and wondering if I could ever do the same.

Last winter the PWD decided to take a new road past my doorstep, and the first casualty was the walnut tree. Along with a large number of different trees growing below the cottage, it fell to the contractors' axes.

Recently when I met the old woman on the road, I asked her, 'Where do you get your walnuts now, Grandmother?'

'Nowhere,' she answered stoically. 'That was the last walnut tree on the hillside.'

WHY I MISS THE GOOD OLD GP WHO KEPT IT SIMPLE

Customs change with the changing times, but not always for the better.

I do miss the old GP, the family doctor, who would turn up at your house at short notice. You had only to give him a ring or send him a message saying you or one of your loved ones was down with the flu or mumps or some mysterious fever, and he'd be around in a jiffy. Years of experience enabled him to make a quick and usually accurate diagnosis and he'd write out a prescription on the spot. If he thought it was something very serious he'd direct you to the nearest hospital. If he was a good doctor, his very presence would make you feel better. He'd put his stethoscope to your chest, feel your pulse, look at your tongue, prod your tummy, and make you breathe deeply and say 'Aaah!' You took his pills religiously, and sooner or later you felt better.

Such doctors are a dying breed. Today, young doctors open smart clinics or join city hospitals, and if you want to see them you must stand in line with dozens of other patients. In spite of all the advances of medical science, sick people multiply by the day and our cities are flooded with nursing homes and diagnostic centres. Strange that in this age of scientific and medical wonders, the world should be sicker than ever.

Diabetes, impotency, heart disease, cancer and various viral infections ensure that our medical services are overstretched. Gone are the days when a worried parent would say 'Send for the doctor'. Now it's 'Go to the doctor' or 'Send for an ambulance'. No one is likely to come and sit by your bedside.

So I miss those doctors, now retired or long gone, who would do just that. There was Dr Jwala Prasad, for instance, a dear man who smoked quite heavily, and who owned one of the three or four cars that plied on the Mussoorie roads back in the 1960s and '70s. He was famous for his phrase 'Nothing to worry about.' No matter how ill you were, in pain or racked with a fever, he'd pat you on the shoulder and say, 'Nothing to worry about. You're going to be fine!'

And it actually helped! Such is the psychology of illness or wellness.

Another friendly neighbourhood doctor who I miss is Dr Bisht. I had only to ring him up, to tell him I was in dire straits, and ten minutes later I would hear the splutter of his old scooter as it drew up below my steps. 'Pulse is a bit fast today,' he'd say, after a brief examination. 'It's the blood pressure again. Don't tell me you have fallen in love again?'

'What's that got to do with it, doctor?'

'Falling in love always raises the blood pressure.'

In his infinite wisdom he'd hit the nail on the head—or the lover on his aching heart. The remedy? A long walk in the woods. 'Keep walking. That will do the trick.' His theory was that a little exercise was the best remedy for most ailments.

Well, the good doctor has long since retired, but the other day I met him when he was enjoying an outing with his grandchildren, and I could see that he was most anxious to do something for my well-being. At eighty, I do still occasionally fall in love, but on this occasion I had nothing to complain of—no dizziness, no irregular heartbeat, no melancholia or other symptoms of the love-sick—just a seasonal cold. So I told him I had a cold.'

'Take plenty of vitamin C,' he advised. 'And drink lots of water.' Well, I have been taking Vitamin C for a week, and I am looking like a lemon, and passed a lot of water, but a cold is a cold and it will go in its own good time.

I haven't been so lucky with dentists. As a small boy I had protruding teeth, so my mother took me to Dr Kapadia in Dehradun, a famous dentist in his time. But a painful prod from one of his instruments resulted in my screaming and kicking him on the shin. 'Take this boy away,' he told my mother. 'Don't bring him here again.' With the result that I still have protruding front teeth.

But it's better than having dentures. I have an elderly actor friend who was given the role of Count Dracula in one of those vampire films which are all the fashion these days. The trouble is, he wears dentures, false teeth, and when he grins or grimaces he doesn't look at all like a vampire.

'You'll never get those teeth into a beautiful neck,' I told him. 'We'll have to do something about them.'

So I took him to one of those street dentists who ply their trade on the outskirts of our pilgrim towns. He took out his file and sharpened my friend's false incisors until they glittered. Our hero looked like a real vampire with the sharpened incisors. But he didn't get the part. On taking the heroine into his arms and attempting to plunge his teeth into her beautiful neck, his dentures shot out and he was left toothless.

As Donald Trump would say: Sad.

WHY I MISS MY LESS-CASH DAYS

In these days of cash rationing, I miss the days when I used to subsist largely on postal money orders. That was back in the days of my youth, when I freelanced from Dehradun, bombarding the country's newspapers and magazines with my articles and short stories. Magazine payments seldom exceeded 25 rupees for a short story, and the publishers often found it more convenient to send these amounts by money order rather than by cheque.

I preferred it too. Better than hanging around in a bank all morning. The postman became a welcome visitor, sometimes a friend. I would sign on a printed receipt, and become the recipient of several crisp new notes, all real money, waiting to be spent. No doubt my friends would be waiting around the corner, eager to celebrate at the nearest chaat shop; but there is nothing like a little money in the pocket to boost the self-confidence of a fledgling writer.

The magazines that sent me this largesse included Sainik Samachar, the Armed Forces Weekly; Chandamama; Shankar's Weekly; The Tribune of Ambala; The Leader of Allahabad; and Baburao Patel's Mother India. Only one or two of these survive.

The Times of India and *The Statesman* were in a slightly higher bracket as far as payments went. These amounts might seem insignificant today, but in 1956, 25 rupees could buy lunches and dinners for a week.

◆

Prem, who runs a little ration shop down the road, still uses postal money order to send remittances to his aged and ailing mother in their village in a remote area of the Garhwal hills. There is no bank in the area, but the village postman makes his way to her door with a few hundred rupee notes. Let's hope he will still be able to do so.

I have always been loyal to the post office, and still use Speed Post for all my correspondence. Stamps have to be paid for in cash, so I must cut down a little on my letters. If the cash problems go on forever, I suppose postage stamps will vanish too, much to the dismay of philatelists in India and the world over, who eagerly look out for the new issues and first-day covers.

I gave up collecting long ago, but the postage stamp is part of our heritage, portraying the country's past and present.

◆

In my effort to keep up with the times I travel occasionally by plane, and the other day I thought I'd do some shopping at one of our major airports. To my dismay, the proffered credit card could not be used, as the systems 'connectivity' was down. I'm not sure what 'connectivity' means (except in the human sense) but apparently it implies some sort of electronic failure. And I hope it isn't a foretaste of things to come. If there is neither cash nor 'connectivity', what do we do for a bar of chocolate or just a magazine with which to pass the time? You just sit patiently in the airport twiddling your thumbs and gazing at your fellow travellers.

Or being gazed at.

I was sitting there meditating, or rather contemplating, when an attractive young woman came up to me and said, 'Excuse me, but are you Bejan Daruwala?'

Now I've been mistaken for various people in my life, but Bejan Daruwala was a new one.

Naturally I was flattered.

'Regretfully, no,' I answered. 'But I can tell your fortune if you like. Just show me your hand and I'll trace your life line, your head line, and your heart line.'

'No, no,' she said hastily. 'It's all right. I just thought you looked like him.'

'I won't charge anything,' I added, as an afterthought; she was probably short of cash. But she had hurried away. I don't think she trusted palmists.

An hour passed, and someone else approached me. A large lady with a small boy.

'It's so nice to see you here,' she says. 'My little boy studies one of your books in class. Will you give him your autograph?'

'Certainly ma'am.' I beam at the bright little boy. 'And what's the name of the book you are studying?'

'Tom Sawyer,' he says.

Dutifully, I sign Mark Twain on a slip of paper. Mother and son go away quite happy.

One of these days someone is going to mistake me for Ruskin Bond.

